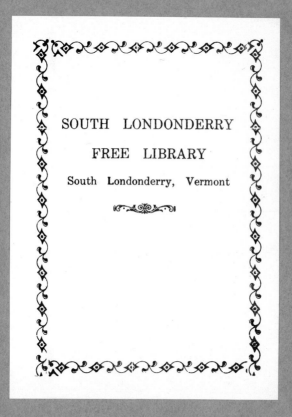

THE REEF GIRL

Books by ZANE GREY

NOVELS

The Reef Girl
Boulder Dam
Blue Feather and Other Stories
The Ranger and Other Stories
Horse Heaven Hill
The Arizona Clan
The Fugitive Trail
Stranger from the Tonto
Lost Pueblo
Black Mesa
Wyoming
Captives of the Desert
The Dude Ranger
The Maverick Queen
The Deer Stalker
Rogue River Feud
Valley of Wild Horses
Shadow on the Trail
Wilderness Trek
Stairs of Sand
Majesty's Rancho
Twin Sombreros
30,000 on the Hoof
Western Union
Knights of the Range
Raiders of Spanish Peaks
West of the Pecos
The Lost Wagon Train
The Trail Driver
Thunder Mountain
The Code of the West
The Hash Knife Outfit
The Drift Fence
Robbers' Roost
Arizona Ames
Sunset Pass
Wild Horse Mesa
The Shepherd of Guadaloupe
Fighting Caravans
Don
Nevada
Forlorn River

The Border Legion
The Call of the Canyon
The Day of the Beast
Desert Gold
The Desert of Wheat
The Heritage of the Desert
The Light of Western Stars
The Lone Star Ranger
The Man of the Forest
The Mysterious Rider
The Rainbow Trail
Riders of the Purple Sage
Tappan's Burro
The Thundering Herd
To the Last Man
The U.P. Trail
Under the Tonto Rim
The Vanishing American
Wanderer of the Wasteland
Wildfire
The Wolf Tracker
Betty Zane
The Spirit of the Border
The Last Trail
The Last of the Plainsmen
The Short Stop—
The Red-Headed Outfield
The Zane Grey Omnibus

OUT-OF-DOOR BOOKS

Zane Grey's Adventures in Fishing
An American Angler in Australia
Tales of Fresh-Water Fishing
Zane Grey's Book of Camps and Trails
Tales of Tahitian Waters
Tales of Fishes
Tales of Fishing Virgin Seas
Tales of Lonely Trails
Tales of Southern Rivers
Tales of the Angler's Eldorado
Tales of Swordfish and Tuna

BOOKS FOR BOYS

Ken Ward in the Jungle
Roping Lions in the Grand Canyon
The Young Forester
The Young Lion Hunter
The Young Pitcher

THE REEF GIRL

by Zane Grey

✷

Foreword by Loren Grey

✷

✷

Harper & Row, Publishers

New York, Hagerstown

San Francisco, London

✷

✷

✷

FIRST EDITION

Designed by Sidney Feinberg

#14848   7/78

Library of Congress Cataloging in Publication Data

Grey, Zane, 1872-1939.
  The reef girl.
  I. Title.
PZ3.G87Rg 1977 [PS3515.R6545]   813'.5'2
ISBN 0-06-011624-2   77-3791

77 78 79 80 81 10 9 8 7 6 5 4 3 2 1

Foreword

Of all the places my father visited in his many travels, I think that, except for the American West, he probably loved Tahiti the most. It was here, after a ten-year odyssey over most of the South Pacific, that he realized one of his greatest ambitions—the first capture of a big game fish over one thousand pounds in weight. It was a giant blue marlin swordfish, a species which many aficionados of the deep-sea angling fraternity consider, even today, to be the greatest fighting fish in all the seas, immortalized by Ernest Hemingway in his classic novel *The Old Man and the Sea*.

But there was so much more to Tahiti than fishing that captivated my father, as it had so many other writers: Stevenson, Melville, Maugham, Nordhoff and Hall, to mention just a few. It was Tahiti's incredible scenic beauty, and the curious mélange of racial and ethnic cultures, that absorbed him almost from the first day he landed. He was intrigued by the superstitious, almost mystical alliance the natives seemed to have with Tahiti's forbidding mountains, her lush abundance, and flashing reefs. As were many writers of his generation, he was fascinated, and yet in some ways repelled by the casualness of the sexual attitudes of the natives, particularly in their relationships with white men. Another theme, his outrage at the way missionaries and other whites took advantage of the Polynesians— as others had done to the Navajo Indians in Arizona and New Mexico—also runs throughout this book as it does so compellingly in *The Vanishing American.*

Though romanticized, *The Reef Girl* is a rather astonishingly accurate view of some of the realities of this culture as it existed in the 1930s. It is not too surprising that, when first submitted for publication shortly after his death in 1939, the novel was rejected as being too "daring" for Zane Grey. But certainly, even by today's standards, it would have to be considered his most modern, and certainly his most unique, novel.

Perhaps I feel a closer kinship personally with this book than with anything else he wrote because I was there with him on several of his expeditions, at a time when much of Tahiti's magnificence was still unspoiled. I have tramped up many of the island's crystal rivers in search of the elusive nato—a wild native bass that, believe it or not, rises to a fly and fights like a trout. Often I have stood near the outer reefs watching the gigantic waves spawned by Antarctic storms crash with monstrous abandon on the living coral. Several times I saw the mysterious nature men, with whom the novel's hero, Donald Perth, lives for several weeks during his travail before his passionate encounter with the Reef Girl. They were white men who had renounced civilization and actually lived in isolation on Tahiti's lonely east coast, far beyond the end of the road.

In *The Reef Girl,* the love story of Donald and Faaone defies both the primitive superstition and savagery of her background and the shabby prejudices of Tahiti's white rulers. It has the sweep and vision that characterize many of Zane Grey's finest Western novels, along with a marvelous sensual, almost mystical, awareness of the oneness of man with nature—a quality which no other author I have ever read has captured with more poetic intensity and passion.

LOREN GREY

Woodland Hills, Calif.

part I
TAHITI

1

❋

❋

❋

Donald Perth awakened with a start from an uneasy sleep. The ship's engines had slowed, and the familiar rolling motion was muted. A gray-rose dawn showed through his porthole. Rising, he went to look out.

The ship was moving at less than half speed, and the smooth sea slid by noiseless as oil. In the east a faint dark line, gradually sloping out of the sea, attested to the island of Tahiti.

He was about to look for his clothes when an unfamiliar fragrance assailed his nostrils. It was ineffably sweet and suggested flowers, summer, cleanliness, and something intoxicating.

"Frangipani!" he exclaimed, pleased that he recognized a perfume that he had never smelled before. Faint as it was, the odor lingered. Donald imagined islands set in lonely seas hot with the breath of the tropics—blossoming trees, wilderness green, streams, lacy waterfalls like downward smoke. This was the incense that had lured Tennyson's Lotos-Eaters.

As long as he could remember, Donald had cherished an unspoken desire to visit the South Seas. In his boyhood he had read Defoe and Stevenson, Melville's *Typee* and the works of Loti, Calderon, Brooks, and Nordhoff and Hall. More recently

Loti, Calderon, Brooks, and Nordhoff and Hall. More recently he had pictured himself going alone to the fabled islands to gather material for his own writing, which up to this time had brought him little but a collection of rejection slips, with, occasionally, a faintly encouraging letter exhorting him to "keep it up—some day you might become a writer." He would travel at his leisure, visit the faraway atolls where the steamers never called, mingle with the natives, and from all of this fashion a romantic novel that would make him famous. But, as with most of his dreams, this one had been doomed to oblivion.

For he was decidedly not alone. When Mrs. Carlson Gannett, his future mother-in-law, had arbitrarily decided that on this voyage, which was to climax her many travels, she should sail to Tahiti in the company of her only daughter Winifred and Winifred's fiancé, he had been unable to refuse. Winifred had been enraptured and adamantly unable or unwilling to understand his objections. So here they were on the RMS *Tahiti*, ready to land at Papeete.

As he recalled the events of the last ten days, since the ship had left San Francisco, his reverie faded into the haunting premonition that had dogged him lately—that somehow this voyage was destined to end disastrously. For the first few days out, he had more or less reconciled himself to his resentment over Mrs. Gannett's imperiousness and Winifred's desire to postpone their wedding until after the trip. But, as the days lengthened and the languor of the tropic sun and the trade winds increased, he had become more and more uneasy. He had always known that Winifred was restless and temperamental and had what seemed a never-satisfied longing for the unusual. And she liked the advances and admiration of men, although before this voyage she had always, as far as he knew, kept them well at a distance. On shipboard, however, many of her inhibitions had apparently fallen away. She had been drinking more heavily than he had ever seen, and was animated, flirtatious, even seductive with a number of the many men who crowded around her.

At first Donald pretended not to notice this. But when her attentions began to focus on the tall bronzed Englishman named T. Bennet-Stokes, who, though handsome and well-preserved, was obviously twice her age, he confronted her and they quarreled bitterly. But the next morning she seemed contrite, promising not to encourage Bennet-Stokes's advances, and at least for a few days things went more smoothly.

Then, last night at the captain's ball, the jealousies had flared once more. The scene was painfully sharp in Donald's mind, as if he were living it again. The blue gown Winifred wore to dinner was new to him. It was cut disturbingly low, revealing her dazzling white shoulders and the fullness of her breasts, to his eyes almost uncontained by the thin folds of the gown. Her long golden hair was piled regally up on top of her head. Clean-cut and small of feature, her oval face was flushed with excitement, and her flashing blue eyes seemed to take in all of the admiring glances that were turned in her direction. Donald resisted the impulse to call attention to the gown. She would have said he was old-fashioned and prudish and done exactly as she pleased anyway. But when Bennet-Stokes approached her after dinner, and she danced with him several times and went out on deck with him at least once, Donald could contain himself no longer.

"You promised you weren't going to encourage him again!" he whispered bitterly, when she sat down at last, and Bennet-Stokes had excused himself.

She was furious. "What am I supposed to do, insult him? Besides, what else is there to do on this tub besides drink and dance? All *you* want to do is walk along the deck and look at flying fish."

"And what does *he* do? Tell you all about the illegitimate half-breed daughter he has on Tahiti?"

Winifred gave him a withering glance, but her retort went unvoiced as her mother, overhearing Donald's speech, cut in:

5

"What did you say, Donald? You don't *believe* that South Sea gossip, do you? The vessel reeks with it."

"That kind of thing is hardly ever gossip down here," Donald answered her. "Anyway, the captain told me the story, and he's actually seen the girl. He says she's an incredibly beautiful Lorelei, who lures white men to her lair and then destroys them. Her name is Faaone."

"How romantic," said Winifred, acidly. "With your notions about the South Seas, Don, she might suit you a lot better than *I* do!"

"Winifred! That's a disgraceful way to talk," her mother exclaimed. "You don't really mean it."

"Maybe I do. I'm fed up with Don being so jealous and trying to boss me around, as if I were a child. I'll do what I damn well please!"

At that sally, Donald excused himself and left the table. He paced the deck, burning with rage but feeling unequal to a confrontation with all the others present. Finally, exhausted, he went to his stateroom and turned in. It was several hours before he could fall asleep.

Now, watching the dawn, he reflected bitterly that he really had been afraid to push her too far in the ugly mood she was in. He was only too well aware that Winifred could have chosen from among many more eligible men than he. She had been left financially independent by her father, and her mother was also wealthy. Donald's income, from a small trust fund left him by his father, was sufficient for him—he was paying his own expenses on this trip—but would be totally inadequate for the luxury to which she was accustomed. This was a galling truth that Donald had found hard to accept, and after graduating from college he had tried several kinds of business jobs. But he had failed at them all, because his ambition was to write. Yet Winifred had seemed happy to have him court her. That she loved him, there appeared to be no reasonable doubt. But for her mother, she would have yielded to his entreaties and mar-

6

ried him long ago. When they were off this damned ship, he thought, and away from civilized distractions, the two of them could be alone together again. Then, perhaps, they could restore the easy, loving intimacy that had characterized their relationship at home.

Donald dressed slowly and went up on deck. Ship hands were unlashing the gangplank. Four bells struck: six o'clock. He was the only passenger up, except for some in the steerage, forward. Rounding to the port side, Donald again faced the light from the east. It was brighter, and there were pink and pearl edges to the clouds. That faint, fringed line had mounted in a few minutes to a black slope that rose and rose incredibly until it disappeared under a canopy of gray. Tahiti with her mountain peaks lost in the clouds! The magnificence of the panorama lifted his spirit immeasurably.

He glued himself to the corner of the rail forward and wished for a thousand eyes. The ship was sliding on. The water murmured from the bow. Now, the smoky clouds in the east let through rifts of the ethereal lights of the sun, still below the horizon. They grew magically in brilliance and color. A thin wandering line of pale reef appeared along the dark land.

When the ship was only two or three miles off the channel, a few passengers, some in pajamas and dressing gowns, came on deck to spoil the silence with their babbling. But Donald scarcely noticed them. He saw only the thirty miles of island slope, a sheer gradual rise from the sea that disappeared halfway up the mountain in the magnificent scroll of cloud which jealously guarded the peaks. He was astounded at its mighty bulk, forbidding and dark, savage and rugged with its canyons, apparently all alone in that vast sea.

Soon the mountain mass towered so high that the ship seemed a tiny crawling thing in its shadow. They were approaching the barrier reef, a white, restless, changeable movement of water against coral. On the other side of it, a pale gleaming lagoon ended in dim lights, gray-hulled schooners, church spires and roofs, tall full-foliaged trees. Papeete. The journey had come to an end.

The bugler passed Donald on his way to rouse the still-sleeping passengers with his brazen notes. Suddenly, despite his grievance, he wanted Winifred. She must see this unparalleled sight. He hurried below to rap on her stateroom door.

"Win, we're here!" he shouted, excited as a boy. "Tahiti! It's grand! Get up!"

Presently she opened the door an inch and peeped out, sleepy-eyed but smiling. "Darling, is it fire or shipwreck?"

"Win, we've arrived!"

"So that's it. All right, darling, I'll be up in a minute. Soon as I'm dressed."

Stifling his disappointment at her evident lack of excitement, Donald rushed back on deck, coming out on the starboard side. He could not see the sun, but he knew from the rosy sheen upon the water that it had risen. The south slope of the mountain dropped sheer to the sea. He saw another island, smaller, ragged in outline, dominated by two mountain spires that were crowned with pearl. That would be Moorea, little sister to the Queen of the Pacific. Like a painted island on a painted sea it held Donald rapt for a moment, until his gaze was drawn to a curving line of surf, coming from the open sea between the islands and sweeping on for a league before ending in a sharp curve. A mighty swell lifted itself out of the heaving blue, to mount and rise, to curl its lofty crest, sunrise-flushed and glorious, to fold over with slow majesty forming a long tunnel down the reef, at last to crash in glittering rose-ruin on the coral, to plunge like the advance guard of an army of wild white horses, and to fall and spread, a wide sheet of foam in the smooth lagoon.

Wild white horses of the sea. He had read that passage somewhere in one of the South Sea books he had devoured. This was the reef surf on the south break of the passage leading into Papeete Harbor. It held Donald spellbound with an inexplicable emotion—not joy, not thrill, not enslavement to beauty, but something deep and terrible out of the depths of him.

Winifred did not put in an appearance until the liner was inside the lagoon and slowing up to anchor for the French officials to come on board for inspection.

"How perfectly lovely!" she cried, her eyes lighting with the scene. She looked appropriately cool in a white silk suit and wide-brimmed straw hat. There was a touch of blue about her, which matched her eyes. And what was characteristic of her, the events of the previous evening appeared to have been totally forgotten.

"Don, look at the stream of bicycles."

"Everybody rides in the tropics."

"It's French, all right. Look at the red roofs. And those trees, Don! I've never seen anything so beautiful!"

"They must be flambuoyants—flame trees. I've read their blossoms color the air and fall to make the ground red."

"What's that smell? It's so sweet! It clogs my nose."

"Frangipani flowers."

"With such color and perfume this island should be paradise."

"I hope we find it so. It will be our fault if we don't." His earnestness made her turn to look at him. Suddenly she was grave, the laughter gone from her eyes.

"Don, I've got the queerest sensation. Not so much a thrill. Almost a sinking feeling instead. I—"

Before she could say more, a steward called all passengers to the dining salon to show their passports and immigration papers. By the time this tedious hour had ended and Donald was free again to look, the ship was on her way to the dock. It glided slowly up to the long wharf, where small boats filled with natives took the ends of the huge hawsers.

A colorful crowd lined the wharf, many of them stevedores waiting to board the ship, and the rest women, dressed in brilliant pink and yellow and red. Gendarmes in uniform paraded the dock; cars rolled up to park at each end of the long wharf;

streams of bicycles and pedestrians flowed down from the main street, where the great full-foliaged trees obscured the buildings; schooners of various sizes were anchored, stern ends to the shore. Frenchmen in white linen, wearing helmets, stood back in the shade of the sloping roof of the copra shed. Another knot of other whites, both men and women, waited expectantly on the dock for passengers to disembark.

Three things struck Donald simultaneously—the bizarre foreign atmosphere, the blistering heat, and the almost overpowering, sickeningly sweet odor of copra. He had never before smelled this important product of the South Sea islands, yet he knew it at once.

Winifred could not stand the heat and drew back in the shade with her mother. Presently the ship was moored fast and the stairway let down. A stream of stevedores came running up, two abreast—shirtless, dark-skinned, muscular young men, chattering in Tahitian. They struck Donald as pleasant, clean looking, carefree. All were barefooted. They had huge callused feet with widespread toes, and, in general, somewhat flat noses and thick lips, evidence of the long-ago visit to Tahiti of fleets of canoes from the New Hebrides. The voyagers had been big men—Melanesians from the far west—and the Tahitian women had been much taken with them, cannibals though they were.

The native women followed the stevedores on board. They were young and old, and some were handsome. All had brown skin and long lustrous brown hair that reached in braids below their waists. Their bare legs were rendered ugly by scars and sores upon the ankles. Most of them, like the men, were barefooted. They wore flowers daintily stuck over their ears, and carried leis—wreaths of blossoms—in their hands. A saucy-eyed girl offered two of these for sale. Donald bought them, one of beautiful white-petalled flowers with yellow centers, and the other of dead-white small blossoms, tightly woven. Close at hand they smelled sickeningly sweet.

"Frangipani?" asked Donald.

The girl nodded with a bright smile and designated the other as "tiare-tahiti."

Donald went in search of Winifred. She was delighted, and could not choose which she liked better. Donald put the lei of tiare-tahiti over her head.

They stood together for a few moments, watching the lively scene. But, as the sun rose higher in the sky, the heat became more and more oppressive, the stench of the copra more pronounced. Finally, Donald said, "Win, I've read that this wharf is the only place on Tahiti that is not delightful. Let's get going."

It developed that baggage had to be transferred to the customhouse, and that the stevedores exacted a wage scarcely commensurate with their brawn. Then, when they had packed their numerous bags and trunks—mostly belonging to Winifred —through the vast, gloomy, suffocating copra storehouse to the barn-like edifice where the customs officials held forth, Donald found he had to pay several more carriers than he had actually engaged. A small case, fortunately not valuable, was not to be located. The baggage had to be opened and the contents displayed; Winifred's delight in exhibiting her finery did not extend to this, and she lost her temper.

Donald asked to be directed to a hotel where they could stay for a day, until desirable lodgings could be found out of town. The hotel was in a back street, and by the time the party reached it, Mrs. Gannett had been reduced to a state of collapse. She refused to go upstairs but sat down instead on the hotel porch, which was an open dining room. The three rooms assigned to them were high-ceilinged, but dingy and poorly furnished. Moreover, they were hot. Donald gave the room with the best bed and the best mosquito net to Winifred, but the gesture did not elicit any gladness from her. She vowed she would be dissolved in another minute.

Donald took her downstairs, where her mother greeted him with, "So *this* is Tahiti!"

"This is Papeete," corrected Donald, "which was never her-

11

alded by any visitors as heaven. I venture to think you'll right-about-face when we get a cottage along the shore."

"Oh, we'll take our medicine, Don," said Winifred. "I'm really thrilled to death. It's only that I didn't expect Tahiti to be like this."

"It will be days before we get used to the heat, I guess, but then it will be better. You stay here while I go get a car."

He returned in an hour with this mission accomplished, and they spent the rest of the morning driving all around the quaint town, with its cosmopolitan population and exotic tropic foliage. Winifred raved over the flambuoyant and the hibiscus blossoms—her favorite color was red—while Mrs. Gannett liked the huge trees and the arbors of bougainvillea. Donald's close contact with the frangipani perfume intoxicated him. Winifred admired the Tahitian men, commenting that they were built like football players.

The Chinese quarter of town interested Mrs. Gannett, who speculated on what could be bought and made in the stores, as they drove south along the beach road. Here, in the breeze and the shade, with the placid many-hued lagoon and the white reef and blue sea seen through the coconut trees, they found the Tahiti of the legends. But they did not find a cottage to rent near the town. So they drove north. On that coast they looked at several, any one of which would have sufficed, but Donald insisted on seeing every available place. It was lunchtime before this could be accomplished, so they returned to the hotel, where Donald, as a precaution, had ordered the meal in advance. They found the French cooking and service more than satisfactory, whatever the shortcomings of the hotel in other respects.

After lunch, while the women rested before continuing the search for a cottage, Donald walked down to the quay. It was so hot that he wanted to sit down at every possible place on the way. When he finally reached the harbor, the stone seats in front of the moored schooners proved too inviting to resist.

12

This was ship day, and of course the big day in Papeete, but Donald found a certain peace. The cars sped by, honking their horns, the bicycles slid along, and the big stores were opening their doors after the midday rest, but no one appeared in a hurry. He tried to talk to natives and found them agreeable, although few were able to understand him. Several Americans from one of the schooners stopped to make his acquaintance. He asked some questions of a young Englishman, who knew the ropes and was courtesy itself. He wandered into several of the curio shops, in one of which he met the American and the New Zealander who ran the place, and who were pleasant and helpful to him. A most affable Chinese in one of the big stores, a merchant who had been years in San Francisco, bade him welcome. From his store Donald strolled across the street into a gaudily painted, noisy café, which was full of natives, sailors, passengers from the ship, and a score or more of handsome Tahitian girls. Soft drinks and refreshments were served, and there was a din of clicking pool balls and animated talk. Donald did not miss the speculative, bold gaze some of the native girls bestowed upon him. When he left this resort he ran into Captain Smollett, the ruddy-faced New Zealand skipper of the RMS *Tahiti.*

"Hello, I was wondering about you," said Smollett. "Are you settled? Have you found some decent quarters?"

"No to all that, Captain," replied Donald. "But we're going to be all right, I'm sure."

"Let's go have a drink. I'm sailing at five, and I may not meet you again." Captain Smollett, with his hand under Donald's arm, led him to Papeete's fashionable French café, the Cercle Bougainville, which was upstairs in a building that faced the lagoon. A wide porch opened directly opposite the steamer at the dock. There were many tables, most of which were occupied. Numerous Frenchmen in white sat quietly drinking their wine, and watching the tourists.

Donald recognized most of his fellow passengers from the

13

voyage down. There were other Americans, too, and a coterie of Englishmen. Captain Smollett appeared to know everyone present. He pointed out two American women, who, he said, lived in Papeete, and a French actress from Paris. She was a handsome hard-featured blonde and was most attentive to a Pomeranian dog she carried. Donald did not see a Tahitian woman there. Gaiety appeared to be the order of the moment, and wine glasses were more in evidence than cocktails. Donald's keen eyes, however, noted a number of hands that shook perceptibly while lifting their glasses. He commented upon this to his host.

"Everybody drinks on Tahiti," Smollett replied. "They have to."

"Why's that?"

"I'm sure I never understood it. But always you hear that most foreigners, except the French, cannot stand Tahiti unless they drink. Some say it's the heat, but I don't think it's that so much as the fact that most people who come to Tahiti to stay for any length of time want to forget. Let me introduce you to some of them."

Of the dozen or more there to whom Captain Smollett presented Donald, all were permanent residents of Tahiti, and half of them were striking in one way or another. He was particularly pleased to meet two American authors with whose books he was familiar. Both had fought in France with the famous Lafayette Esquadrille; gassed and shell-shocked, they had sought the peace of the tropics. Donald divined that they had found it, and a wholly unexpected fame from their writings as well. He was introduced to the American wife of an English official stationed at Papeete, a charming and cultured woman. She seemed eager for news of home, for which she asked with wistful eyes. Two other Americans, one a yachtsman from San Francisco and the other an artist, greeted Donald as if he were a long-lost friend.

Lastly Donald met the Bellairs, who were especially agreeable to him. John Bellair was a blond New Englander, not much over thirty, whose handsome clean-cut face bore shadows and lines which belied his youth. He wore white linen shorts that revealed his brown muscular legs. Catherine, his wife, seemed younger and had regular features and a most gracious manner. Donald met their overtures of friendship with something akin to surprise at the enthusiasm with which these exiles from America welcomed someone fresh from its shores. They let him go reluctantly, with assurances that they would show Tahiti to him and his friends.

As he and Captain Smollett left the café, Donald noticed a shining black seven-passenger sedan parked a few steps out from the pavement. The door to the rear seat was open, and a woman leaned out of the front seat talking in rapid French to a man Donald soon recognized as Bennet-Stokes. Her eyes were big and dark, and they blazed with hate, if Donald had ever seen it. Bennet-Stokes stood with his back to the pavement, his hands spread deprecatingly.

Suddenly a girl emerged from the store next door, followed by a Chinese boy carrying packages.

"By Jove—Faaone!" ejaculated the Captain.

One glance was all Donald needed to realize that he had never seen such a creature in all his life. With the lithe grace of a tigress, she stepped past Bennet-Stokes, who had turned. She passed him without a glance of recognition, her small, dark head held up as regally as that of an empress.

"Faaone!" called Bennet-Stokes. "Here! I want to talk to you. I've come all the way from London."

She turned her back on him and stood beside the car door, while the boy deposited his load of bundles inside. She wore a dress as scarlet as the flambuoyant blossoms overhead. Donald's gaze swept from her crown of magnificent black hair, which shone with a lustrous gleam, to her slim bare legs and small feet, slippered in red, and back to her face. It was oval in shape, its hue a gold tan, and exceedingly beautiful, with sweet, bowed lips as red as her dress, and lighted by great dusky eyes, unfathomable and compelling, that seemed on fire with passion. Her figure was voluptuous, yet slender. As Donald continued to gaze at her, she looked up to encounter his eyes. She looked him up and down, then at Captain Smollett, nodding in recognition, and then flashed her eyes back upon Donald. Suddenly she smiled. What an extraordinary transformation! A lovely warmth supplanted the dignity and passion in her face. It became that of a curious girl, pleased by admiration. Then, as Donald's pent-up feeling was liberated in an involuntary shuddering expulsion of breath, Faaone entered the car, closed the door, gave him another quick dusky glance, and leaned back out of sight. The woman in the front seat spoke to the native driver. She took no further notice of Bennet-Stokes, who stood there as the car moved away, his face pale with anger. Finally, after the car had disappeared he strode away down the street.

"Well, what did you think of that, Perth?" exclaimed Captain Smollett. "That you and I should see the meeting of Stokes, his one-time vahine, and their daughter Faaone! If I'm not a fool he wants that girl. But did he get the brush-off! What did you think of her?"

"I—I don't know," replied Donald, unsteadily.

"Didn't you think she was pretty?"

"Pretty doesn't describe it. She's magnificent! A savage princess!"

"Yes. And she was quick to see that you thought so. These Tahitians like sincerity. All they've ever gotten from most white men is to be cheated . . ." The Captain paused, then turned to Donald with outstretched hand. "Well, Perth, I'll bid you farewell. Remember my advice. Don't stay here too long."

"Goodbye, Captain. Thanks for your kindness. I'll not forget you."

Donald stood alone, staring down the street, with its passing throng of variegated colors, its cars and bicycles, and the blazing white sunlight in such vivid contrast to the green and red of the flambuoyant trees. He did not want to move, to return to the hotel, where he was long overdue. He thought of Winifred, and it occurred to him that the significance of this encounter with Faaone lay in the fact that he would never tell Winifred about it.

2

❋

❋

❋

Donald lay in his hammock under the flambuoyant tree with the most absolutely pleasant sensation that he had ever known.

Two miles north of Papeete, far from the road and close to the beach, they had found two cabins, ideal in every way. The larger house was modern, with running water and electric light, two bedrooms and a shower, and a spacious porch opening right on the lagoon. The small structure, Donald's cottage, was made of coconut palm and bamboo, a primitive abode that let sunlight and air into its one room, as well as the rain that blew in upon the porch where he slept. A big low-branched flambuoyant tree, more copiously covered with scarlet blossoms than with lacy fern-like leaves, shaded the porch and hammock with a rosy hue. Frangipani trees, in full and fragrant flower, and hibiscus bushes, blooming red and purple and lilac, banked the shore side of the main cottage. Gold and green palms leaned gracefully toward the sea, their long leaves hanging and rustling. There were other trees, the names of which Donald had not yet learned. The beach was fine black lava sand sloping to the lagoon, from which came the gentle and continual lap, lap, lap of waves. Offshore a few rods, dark bronze and amber coral

18

gleamed just under the surface. The beach curved a little outwards to the end of a neck of land, green-swarded and covered with a park-like grove of widely separated coconut palms, through which could be seen Venus Point, a cape some miles to the north. Seaward, however, the view from the porches of both cottages was open. Beyond the half mile of placid blue lagoon beat and crawled and heaved the white reef, the eternal surf forever breaking on the coral with its varied music, from low murmur and hollow splash to boom and thundering roar. Beyond it, the dark-blue, white-ridged sea moved, blown always by the trade wind that lulled or raged according to its mood. Moorea stood up across the channel like a cameo, clean-cut at dawn, shrouded in pearl and gold clouds at sunset— marvelously lovely at that hour—and never the same. It relieved the glare of the sea; it broke the endless horizon; it collected clouds all day long, as if its purpose was to give the sun infinite power at the end of day.

The few days since Donald had installed Winifred, her mother, and himself here had made time seem as if it had not been. They had rested; with the vanishing of the memory of discomfort had come a sheer joy of being, of seeing, and feeling. Here, on the porch of her cottage, Mrs. Gannett was happy to sit and do nothing, except tell Winifred and Donald repeatedly and with great satisfaction that this was why she had insisted on coming to Tahiti.

"Mom, darling, Don and I crawl," Winifred would reply lazily. "We bless you for dragging us here. It's paradise!"

Winifred, too, seemed unutterably contented, sweeter than Donald had ever known her. As he had hoped, getting away from the ship and Papeete had brought back the closeness they shared at home. The nameless dread he had felt aboard ship was gone.

Hearing a slight sound, he turned. Winifred was approaching. She was clad, or rather unclad, as he had never before seen her. The blue shorts she wore were most aptly named, and her only upper garment was half of a blue silk scarf, which thinly covered her full breasts and was knotted tightly behind her back. Already her satin skin had begun to warm in the generous sunshine. Donald started up, surprised not so much by this sight of his fiancée as by the fact that secretly he wondered how Faaone would look in such attire. The comparison did not favor Winifred, although she was slimly and elegantly formed and possessed white unblemished skin.

"Where did you get that outfit?" he inquired lazily.

"Don't I look sharp? I bought it in Hollywood. This is standard dress on the beaches."

"Undress, you mean, darling. What's the sequel?"

"Eve in a fig leaf, and a lot of Adams around."

"Not while this Adam's on hand."

"Don, you're such a prude."

"No—jealous, darling." He drew her down beside him on the hammock.

"Don! You do have faith in me, don't you?" she asked softly.

"Of course. If I hadn't, I wouldn't love you."

"But men love women they have no faith in."

"Not love."

"I think I love you more here than I did at home. Tahiti is so lovely, darling. Let's never leave."

"Win, you'll tire of it in three months."

"Damn it, Don!" She jumped up, nearly turning him out on the floor. "When I say something in earnest I always get that sort of a reply. You have no faith in me—to you I'm just a butterfly."

"Well, you're a beautiful one at least. Where are you off to?"

"I'm going to wade along the shore, out on the coral."

"I'll go with you," he called after her, then leaped up to follow her retreating figure. "Win, I know I told you the Tahitians said sharks never come into this bay, but I've heard that last year, below Papeete, a woman was attacked by a shark while she was in bathing. It was only a little one—scarcely three feet long—

20

but it stripped all the flesh off her arm as she fought it, and she nearly died of blood poisoning. Don't trust this shore to bathe, except in some coral-protected place. And *don't* cut yourself on the coral."

"Don't—don't—don't! I declare you're worse than Mother. Tahiti has no sharks or snakes or reptiles. Nothing to be afraid of! And no conventionality, either! Nobody who cares a damn who you are or what you do! I love it!"

They walked up and down the slow-sloping beach, gathering tiny shells and bits of strange sea flotsam. Then they waded out upon the amber shelf of coral, which was half a hundred feet wide and extended along the shore around the point. The tide was low, and there was only six inches of water, except when a heave from the lagoon sent a slow-breaking wave over the fringe. These crashed melodiously and sent a creamy ripple seething and singing toward the shore, to foam up to their knees and evoke cries of delight from Winifred. In the intervals between these miniature breakers, they hunted shells on the coral. Winifred had sharp eyes for such work, and she found beautiful tiny ones embedded in holes. They were mostly cowries of two varieties, one pale violet or lilac in hue and the other larger, green-gold in color, with a triangular mark of purple in the center. Donald was more entranced by the moving glints of gold and blue at his feet—tiny fish, scarcely more than an inch long, and very curious or friendly.

They waded along the coral as far around the point as they could go, up to a high sandy beach. Beyond this was a grove of trees upon which fish nets hung, and palm-thatched huts sitting picturesquely in the shade. Tahitians in red pareus sat watching them, and naked children, brown as autumn leaves, paddled and shrieked along the edge of the water. Winifred evinced a lively interest and went close to where the coral ledge ended. It irritated Donald to see that she was as unconscious of her appearance here as she would have been at home, apparently unaware of the effect she had on the watching villagers.

21

The sun seemed hotter than ever as they turned to wade back to their cottages. Suddenly a gray pall swooped down off the mountain and rain came roaring over the palms to fall on the water like dancing pearls. The drops were like bits of ice, a sharp contrast to the warm sea. Then, as suddenly, the shower roared away, out over the lagoon, across the sea, to obliterate Moorea in gray obscurity. The sun blazed out again. Diamond drops fell from the leaves. The glistening green foliage and the bright flowers were renewed. A hot breath, like steam, floated off the land, and like magic all was dry again, even the drenched garments of the waders.

Donald had to carry Winifred forcibly off the coral—she wanted to stay out there in the glorious light and heat. She shrieked with laughter, and when he let her down at the foot of her porch in the shade of the palms and blossoming trees, she kissed him impulsively. He picked her up again and carried her on up the high porch steps.

"Heavens!" Mrs. Gannett exclaimed from her reclining cane chair. "You two seem to have gone native already!"

"Mother, we have come from a false world into a human one," declared Winifred.

"You mean, child, from a civilized world into a savage one. Your costume, if it justifies such a term, is disgraceful."

"To whom? Not to Don. Nor to the natives. Do you know, Mother, I never really felt the sun? We don't *have* sun at home. I should be ready to melt, but, instead, I want to run along the beach like those native kids, I want—" She broke off suddenly.

"I don't know whether bringing you here was such a good idea," said her mother. "Don, will you take your shower first?"

Dinner was not served until seven, one of the few customs Mrs. Gannett was able to preserve at Tahiti. That suited Donald, hungry though he was, for it left the hour of sunset and afterglow to leisurely enjoyment. This would be the seventh sunset over Moorea for him, and he wondered if he could transcribe his impressions to paper. Yielding to the thought, he unpacked his notebook and repaired to a seat against a tree on the point, out of sight of the cottage.

But there the hour passed in enchantment. Donald forgot about his notebook. He would not have lost a second of the wonderful transfiguration, even to write. He was lost in a splendor of gold and rose, blazing at first, too severe for the gaze of man, changing, softening, darkening into sudden twilight and a tranquil dusk. The light left on the lagoon seemed unearthly, something that had never shone on sea or land. The trade wind had faded with the sunset; only a low moan from the reef floated across the glassy expanse; a swish and murmur of gentle ripples came from the fringing coral, and the lap on the sand was scarcely audible.

With a sigh, Donald gave up trying to record what he had seen and understand what he felt. He put away his notebook and went in to supper.

Winifred looked charming in a silken garment, against whose pale hue her tanned arms and flushed face glowed in effective contrast. She was gay and chattered as incessantly as hunger would permit. The dinner was very good, the fish—"pihirias," Chang Loo, the cook, called it—delectable, and the fruit, mangoes, delicious. There were both wild and cultivated mangoes growing on Tahiti, Loo explained, and this was the latter, a large gold-centered fruit, juicy and with a distinctive flavor.

"I've read that it's best to go slow on Tahitian fruits," said Donald, "but we'll try them all—passion fruit, breadfruit, guavas, papayas, all kinds of bananas, fei, and what else I can't remember. The wild oranges are grand! No wonder California won't permit them in the country! And there are other things besides the fruits to try. Yams taste like our sweet potatoes, I hear. We must sample them, and tarts, too. They say we should eat very little meat, but I'm keenest on the seafood anyway. The natives eat centipedes, crayfish, crabs, lobsters, oysters—and octopus!"

"Don! You don't mean that, do you?" queried Winifred.

"Sure. Soaked in lime juice and eaten raw, they say octopus is delicious."

"I thought I'd try anything once, but raw octopus! No, thank you—you'd have to be a savage."

"Well, I wouldn't mind that, if we could get back to civilization now and then."

They sat out on the porch until a mosquito or two drove Mrs. Gannett inside. Then Donald and Winifred set out to walk along the beach. The air was cool, and the scent of the sea, faintly impinging upon the heavy fragrance of frangipani flowers, enhanced its intoxicating power. Along the shoreline reaching out to Venus Point, there were fires of red-burning coconut hulls, and on the reef the bobbing lights of fishermen could be seen. The boom of the surf came distinctly on the soft breeze. Behind the lofty peaks, a silver radiance appeared and began, gradually, to lighten the gloom on the sea. The twang of a guitar and the melancholy chant of a native woman lent the island shore reality.

They walked until they were tired, then wandered back to the cottages. The lights were out in Mrs. Gannett's room when they returned. They sat on the porch steps of the main cottage and watched the moon soar up from behind the Diadem Mountain. A vast greenish white orb, it illumined all open space with an unreal light, and where shadows should have been dark they were gray and translucent.

"Gorgeous! Unimaginable! This beauty—this fragrance—and something else—I don't know what," murmured Winifred, her bare arms going around Donald's neck.

3

❀

❀

❀

One day followed another, the same yet always different, fleeing away in the gladness of children—in the sun, the breeze, the rain, the marvel of sunset and night, in the physical delights of Tahiti.

Donald preferred to lie in the shade and give himself up to the dream and glory of Tahiti and to the novel he was plotting. Winifred liked to bask in the sun and sleep in the shade, too, but she gravitated more to action than did Donald. She liked to play with the children along the beach, to talk to the women and even to the men . . . if casual chance offered. In her walks—Donald did not want her to go alone, so almost always he accompanied her—they went up the beach around the point because Winifred preferred to go that way. Her idea was to try out the Tahitian they had learned on the natives in the village. It was fun and got her further along, she said. And it was true that after a few weeks she could converse fairly well. Her skin colored to a warm tan, and she made a ravishing picture in her abbreviated costumes. She knew that no dress she owned set her beauty off so effectively.

It so happened one afternoon that Donald, lagging behind

Winifred after one of these walks, got back to find several visitors on the porch, among them the Bellairs and Bennnet-Stokes, who was deeply engrossed with Winifred. Donald felt once more the stirrings of jealousy at the way the Englishman seemed to devour Winifred with his eyes.

"Mr. Stokes, I saw your daughter, Faaone, a few weeks ago," he broke in abruptly. "She most certainly is beautiful—by any standards. If she were *my* child, I'd want not only to educate and otherwise take care of her, but to show her off at home."

While the others looked blank, Bennet-Stokes flushed ever so little at Donald's remark. Then he laughed.

"If you stay on Tahiti awhile you'll understand the absurdity of such an idea, as I do," he replied, blandly. "I sent Faaone to school in New Zealand for ten years, but it didn't seem to change her much. She still prefers to stay here with her people. Half-breeds are always ninety-nine percent native. They are simple, fun-loving, physical creatures, to whom drinking and eating, singing and making love are all of life. A native woman likes nothing better than to have a white child—a white pickaninny, as she calls it."

"Just animals, eh?" inquired Donald, sarcastically.

"Precisely. Education and religion are wasted upon native women."

"They have no souls?"

"Souls? Perth, I fear you've been listening to the missionaries or reading some of those endless romantic novels about Tahiti."

"Both. But, really, do you English and Europeans grant Tahitians the possibility of a higher intelligence?"

"I've never even heard it discussed by an Englishman. As for the French, they don't rate Polynesians any higher than the Chinese."

"And the Americans?"

Well, they talk a good bit about it, but I don't suppose at bottom they are much different from the rest of us. American sailors and adventurers certainly consider them merely as playthings, to have their pleasures with and leave."

"It's presumptuous, maybe, for me to say so on such short acquaintance, but I believe Tahitians do have souls, just as we do," declared Donald.

"You *would!*" put in Winifred. "If there were any attribute under the sun denied these natives by explorers and historians, you'd say they had it."

"Mr. Perth is an idealist," said Bennet-Stokes. "But, if he stays here much longer, he'll find out things aren't the way his romantic little stories read. Oh, I concede that a few white men say they love their so-called native wives. Perhaps some of them are telling the truth. But few indeed would actually marry one."

At this point, seeing Donald bent on further argument, Winifred changed the subject, and after a little more talk the visitors strolled off toward their cars. But when they had departed, she took up the discussion again.

"Don, it certainly seems that Bennet-Stokes rubs you the wrong way," she remarked.

"And he doesn't you?"

"No. That was a nasty dig you gave him about Faaone."

"I don't agree with you," replied Donald vehemently. "Somebody ought to tell that smooth-talking lecher where to get off. It was plain to me that he made no distinction whatever between you and Faaone."

"Oh? And how do you get that?" queried Winifred, a dangerous glint in her eye.

"It's obvious you're just another potential conquest to him. Beautiful as hell and superficially sophisticated, but really only another seduction to add to his string. I can tell that just by the way he looks at you."

"Donald Perth, if a man can get such a kick just out of looking at me, he's welcome to it," she retorted defiantly.

"That's quite obvious," said Donald, "*if* that's all there is to it."

They were interrupted at this point by Mrs. Gannett summoning Winifred to dress for dinner and commanding Donald to do the same. No more was said, but Donald was left a prey to vagaries of gloomy thought.

Depression had seldom fastened upon him at home, except in the early hours before dawn, when vitality is lowest. It gripped him here, however, much more often. At home he had fought such spells, soon to rally from them. Here, despite the beauty that surrounded him, the energy, if not the incentive, was wanting. He even took a kind of pleasure in despondency. He had a weary contempt for himself, a suspicion that men like Stokes regarded Winifred as fair game, a foreboding that human nature instinctively and unconsciously sought its lowest level in this strange country of sun and open space.

As he brooded, Donald watched the changing panorama of sky and sea. Behind him the peaks were manteled in gray storm clouds. Rain pattered in the coconut leaves—big, glistening, heavy drops. The descending veils scarcely reached the zone of shore and lagoon. Out at sea, purple and gold clouds were beginning to subdue the brilliance of the sinking sun. He became aware presently of the marshalling of trade-wind clouds along the horizon and a heightening of the sunset hues. The crown of rolling cloud-scroll over Moorea split to let in the fan-shaped rays of sunlight. The canyons could be seen clearly through a lilac haze, and the rugged slopes up to the hidden peaks burned as if with fire. North and west of Moorea the sun was setting behind a magnificent ordinance of skysails, which opened presently for the blazing orb, like a molten vase, to bridge the slender breach of blue. Then the sun began to slide into the sea, and every second the radiance of rifts and cloud-edges lost something of fire. Soon, it was only a red disc above the horizon, paling, sinking, until suddenly it vanished. And just as suddenly sky and sea darkened, and, out of the black array of clouds, night appeared to troop across the waste of water.

Donald's mood, too, had changed. All his gloom had vanished. He found himself wondering how many million times this sunset had taken place since Tahiti emerged from the sea. When had life appeared in the water, and how many million more years had passed till it appeared on the land? The Polynesians seemed to have the secret of life. They were devoid of the introspection that beset men such as himself. They were far closer to the elements, to the creatures from which they had sprung, than his own people. Donald felt that his dark reflections had been a waste of thought. If his mind must work, why not on the phenomenon he had just seen, or on all the physical beauty so marvelously prodigal in Tahiti? Suddenly, he saw clearly that peace, health, even rapture abided in unthinking sensorial perception. Aware that rational thought would repudiate this notion, he nevertheless felt that he had discovered the primal allure of the South Seas.

4

❋

❋

❋

On the following night, Winifred decided to dress in the elaborate formal creation that had been so much admired on the ship, and for once Donald did not fret at being kept waiting. The longer the slow process took the less time there would be for the party at the Bellairs' and the ball at the Colonial Club afterward.

They arrived late for the party, which was held on a level sward near the beach, in a grove of palms. While Winifred complained that her high-heeled slippers were not intended for walking, and Mrs. Gannett hoped the threatening shower would hold off until they were safely under a roof, Donald was caught up by something raw and exotic in the scene they were approaching. Lamps with yellow flares lighted the lawn; the roll of drums, quick, incessant, punctuated periodically by an abrupt bang, was unlike anything he had ever heard.

Evidently the moment was a rest between dances. Groups of natives lined the glade, and in front of them chairs had been placed for white guests, of whom there were many. The dancers, recognizable by their yellow hula garb, crowded round a table loaded with a huge punch bowl, bottles, and boxes. Hilarity was rampant.

Bellair met Donald and his party. "We've kept chairs for you," he told them.

"Are we too late?" asked Winifred.

"No, if you can take it hot right off," was Bellair's rather enigmatic reply, and he laughed in his easy way.

When the party got to their seats, Donald saw that Bennet-Stokes was next to Winifred. The gown she wore, which had so captivated the Englishman on shipboard, apparently had not lost its appeal, and she was keen, gay, flashing-eyed, responsive to the situation. Most assuredly she was thinking, as well, what effect she would have on others, including her fiancé. For the rest she was subject to the excitement of color, movement, talk —to something as subtly pervasive as the fragrance of frangipani flowers and the fact that white people had gathered here to watch the sex dance of the natives.

Presently thirty dancers took places a few feet apart, fifteen girls on one side and the same number of men on the other. They made a picturesque group. The men wore only hula skirts; the girls wore longer hula skirts and halters of the same material, embroidered in red. Some of the girls were handsome, even to Donald's critical eye. The place, the light, the warmth, all contributed to their attraction—dark faces, dark eyes, dark hair, and the slowly swaying forms voluptuously waiting for the music.

At a shout the drums began to roll and boom, and the thirty forms came alive with barbaric rhythm. If it were a dance, it was with the bodies mostly, for while arms and legs moved— kept time—the hips and abdomens quivered, shook, heaved, and swayed from side to side.

"Just look at that one," cried Winifred, in Donald's ear. "Isn't he magnificent?"

Donald had been wholly absorbed by the girls. Now he

31

looked at the leader Winifred designated. He was a young native of lofty stature, in fact the most perfectly built man Donald had ever seen. What mighty legs with great muscles rippling! His shoulders were wide, his hairless chest a great bronze-ridged shield.

The interest of the whites, especially Winifred's, drew the attention of the giant Tahitian, and he weaved toward her until he was scarcely six feet away. To Donald there was something barbaric, even appalling, about him. He shook his powerful frame as the wind shakes the aspen leaves; his lithe hips heaved under the hula skirt like waves of the sea; his brawny arms were spread wide. In the lustful glare of his great eyes, in the contortions of his face, in the tremendous violence of his movements there was a significance no woman or man could fail to catch. Much more than the others, he possessed the diabolic power to represent nature at its most primitive. As the dance rolled and boomed to a climax, Donald thought the man would shake himself to pieces. But when the drums banged the finale, he ceased his gyrations instantly and backed away, graceful and stealthy on his bare feet.

Donald sat a moment, under the dominance of a passion that frightened and maddened him at the same time. Suddenly he wanted to kill that god-like South Sea native, to plunge a bayonet through his leonine loins! He shook himself. What a hellish thought to succumb to! After all, it was only a dance. He leaned across Mrs. Gannett to address Winifred: "What did you think of—that?" he asked, a little huskily.

"Oh, marvelous," she babbled. "They can really dance—such fantastic rhythm, such perfect timing!"

"I mean the big one."

"Rather frightful at such close proximity," replied Winifred, with a laugh. She was pale under her makeup, and her eyes glowed with a dark and mysterious brilliance. Donald felt divided between relief at her indifference and shock at the depth of his own feelings. Most decidedly she was not shocked. She

32

had enjoyed the hula dance, but she might not have been a woman for all the consciousness of its significance that she betrayed.

"That big man—the leader—his name is Tavarie," interposed Bennet-Stokes, leaning toward Winifred and Donald. "He's quite a man among the natives, especially the girls. His father was a chief called the Sweet-Scented Man—he also was fatal to women. If I remember the story, his long-suffering neighbors rebelled and killed him. I saw his skull somewhere, once. Caved in above the ear! Anyway, Tavarie is his son. He's had some affairs with white women—Americans, I imagine. French women never look at natives, and Englishwomen rarely visit Tahiti."

"Sweet-Scented Man—how interesting," murmured Winifred.

About ten o'clock the party came to an end, and most of the guests left for the Colonial ball in Papeete, which was already under way when they arrived. Bright lights and gay music penetrated the flowery foliage that surrounded the clubhouse, a French villa with spacious porches on two sides, where many guests sat at tables drinking. Wide-open doors permitted glimpses of the dancers inside.

Seats were at a premium, and Donald's party was separated at last from the Bellairs and Bennet-Stokes, which did not cause Donald any regrets. A French officer, in a white, gold-decorated uniform, found chairs for them at the table of a Colonel Hendricks, an English army officer. The decorations on his coat attested to his position. His wife was a statuesque brunette with serene poise and several necklaces of pearls and diamonds. Donald had heard about the couple—she was an Italian princess who had married her distinguished husband for love; they had been sojourning in Tahiti for a month. They were most cordial; Winifred and Mrs. Gannett exchanged pleasantries with them on Tahiti—the climate, the natives. Donald listened halfheartedly while he looked about him. The Bellairs, with Bennet-

33

Stokes, occupied a table nearby. Next to them sat a rather hard-featured, flashily dressed American woman, with four French officers in attendance. Donald had heard that she was the wife of a well-known American playwright, rich in her own right and, even in Papeete, conspicuous for her drinking.

"Don, let's dance," demanded Winifred, suddenly claiming his attention.

Winifred loved to dance, perhaps as much for the joy of it as the always manifest admiration she received. And Donald was good at it—she had declared more than once that his dancing abilities had not been the least of the attractions that won her. He assented readily, and they excused themselves and entered the ballroom to join the whirling couples.

"Don, you could dance in your sleep," said his fiancée, after a few minutes, "but, for goodness sake, stop staring at all the pretty girls on the floor. Although, I must admit, some of them are stunning. They must be the girls of the Tahitian-French elite we heard about, who are never seen on the street."

"Win, I never see any other girl when I have you in my arms," he protested. "What man could?"

But, he admitted to himself, he had noticed them. Nor were they averse to his admiring glances. Several were very young, not over eighteen. Their gowns had a French cut that would have graced any function, and inclined to rose and red in color. Most of them wore a hibiscus or flambuoyant flower over one ear.

All too soon the dance ended. "Don, I'm hot," declared Winifred. "Let's go back outside."

They returned to the porch, to be intercepted by Bennet-Stokes.

"Miss Gannett, you dance beautifully," he said gallantly. "Will you honor me with the next?"

"Thank you, yes, if Don doesn't mind," replied Winifred, turning to him as they reached their table. Donald bowed his acquiescence stiffly, unable wholly to hide his displeasure at

34

Winifred's willingness still to accept Bennet-Stokes's attentions.

Bennet-Stokes held Winifred's chair for her. As she seated herself, Donald felt a slight change in the atmosphere at the table. He imagined it might be due to his evident awkwardness over the situation and made an effort to regain his poise.

"Colonel Hendricks, of course—or do you know Mr. Bennet-Stokes?"

"Ah, yes, thank you," replied the Colonel casually, with a slight inclination of his head. But he did not even glance at Bennet-Stokes, whose face turned a dull red. The princess leaned toward Winifred: "You and your fiancé dance beautifully together. It was a pleasure to watch you. Americans are much given to dancing, are they not?"

"Oh, indeed—yes. We love it," replied Winifred hurriedly. She had been as quick as Donald to catch the snub. The Hendrickses obviously knew Bennet-Stokes, and Donald, gazing down at Winifred's flushed face, realized that for once she regretted accepting his attentions.

Finally, Mrs. Gannett broke the silence by addressing herself to the Colonel, and conversation among the four seated at the table was resumed. Donald turned to say something to Bennet-Stokes, but his good intention was thwarted by Stokes's sibilant intake of breath, like the hiss of a snake. He was no longer paying any attention to Donald or the Hendrickses. His eyes were fastened on a party of newcomers, which had entered the room and was being seated by attendants at a table reserved in the corner. Two French officers were accompanied by ladies in white. The younger one looked directly at Donald with great midnight eyes.

"Faaone!" he whispered, as if to himself. The other woman, Donald realized, was her mother.

Faaone's slight smile of recognition, barely distinguishable, inspired Donald to unmastered impulse. To dance with her would more than pay Winifred in her own coin. The girl, meeting his look, answered its intensity. Faaone's mother spoke to her, and then again, evidently without being heard. The Frenchman stared politely. Winifred spoke to him; then her eyes flashed upon Faaone. The slight curl of her red lips thinned out.

Faaone drew Donald irresistibly. It was as if some new, previously unsuspected part of himself had stepped out, for whom this girl was waiting. He found himself making excuses to Winifred and Mrs. Gannett. He walked past Bennet-Stokes and bowed to Faaone's escort.

"Monsieur, I am Donald Perth," he said. "Will you do me the honor to present me to Mademoiselle Faaone?"

There must have been something about the situation that pleased and intrigued the French officer, for he outdid the usual impetuous gallantry of his class. He rose, as did his comrade, to greet Donald in good English and introduce him with a deep bow to the Tahitian girl.

As the music started once more, Donald bowed to Faaone. "Mademoiselle Faaone, will you dance with me?"

"Yes, Monsieur," she replied softly, and rose with panther-like grace to put her hand on his arm.

Inside the ballroom door, Faaone looked up at him as she slipped into his arms. They fell into the rhythm of the dance, as if they had melted into one person.

"Did you do it on his account or hers?" she asked.

"Do what?"

"Ask me to dance—with respect?"

"I only asked for an introduction and a dance according to the custom in my country."

"Men—at least Englishmen or Frenchmen—do not approach me that way, here in Tahiti."

"I am an American. I would have approached you just the same anywhere, and if I had come alone."

"Then I love you for it," she said intensely.

Donald did not know how to take that or answer it. Though he had accepted the character of harlot for Faaone, as it had been told him, the fact of it had not stayed in his consciousness, and he could not see why she should recall it by speaking as she had. But the awkward moment passed, overcome by the sheer ecstasy of their dancing. Only among professionals had Donald ever encountered a girl with Faaone's marvelous lightness of foot and fairy-like grace. She was like thistledown floating in the air, as if to escape from his eager hands. Yet the feel of her was also warm, exotic, sweet as the frangipani flowers in her dusky hair.

"You dance well," she said, after a time, "better than any white man I ever knew."

"Thanks. I wish I had words to tell you how wonderfully you dance."

"I am Tahitian. Have you heard about me?"

"Yes," he replied, "from Captain Smollett."

"You know Benstokes is my father?" she queried.

"You mean Bennet-Stokes, the Englishman at my table just now?" Donald knew of course, but her question, her dark gaze, confused him.

"Yes. He has come back to Tahiti for me, but I shall not go with him. I hate him. There, he is dancing with your sweetheart."

"She has a will of her own," replied Donald, stung by a note of scorn in her voice. "I couldn't prevent it."

"She is very beautiful, as the Tahitians say. They very much admire fair women. But—" She paused and looked intensely up at Donald. "You do not love her as you should."

This time Donald's composure was jolted enough to make him miss his step. "What do you mean?" he demanded.

"I feel it. I can tell when men—white men—love their vahines. Do not keep her out here in Tahiti very long."

"Why not?"

"She cannot stand our sun."

"She'll stay as long as she pleases," he said, almost defiantly.

"But if you are going to marry her—"

"I am. And afterwards she will do what she wants to, just as she does now. American girls won't be bossed."

"They would be better for it, perhaps."

Before he could think of a response to this, the music stopped and the dance was over. Donald's irritation also passed as he looked down at the lovely woman in his arms.

"Faaone, your beauty and grace take my breath away. I would have liked that dance to last forever."

"I, too," she murmured.

"Let's cross—go out on the terrace," suggested Donald. She assented readily, and he led her past the other couples toward the door. Although several of the girls had smiles of greeting for Faaone, there were white women who gazed straight ahead, cold as stone. As for the men, as far as Donald could tell, they would all have liked to exchange places with him.

The very last couple, near the door, happened to be Winifred and Bennet-Stokes. He did not seem comfortable confronting his daughter, but Winifred, without revealing any inner feelings, gave Donald a nod and Faaone a bright admiring smile. Then Donald, with Faaone on his arm, passed out the door to the terrace and into the fragrant and flowering garden beyond.

The trees were silver and white in the moonlight, and the balmy air filled with the incense of tropic flowers. As they walked down the path, he plucked a frangipani blossom and, exchanging it for the one in her hair, put hers in his buttonhole. He did not touch her, yet never in his life had he been so alive to the nearness and excitement of a woman.

Aside from a few questions, he was silent. She told him how Bennet-Stokes had sent her from Tahiti to be educated in New Zealand, when she was a child. She had returned to the island at fifteen.

"It would have been better if I had not been educated," she said bitterly. "I learned in New Zealand how the white men treat natives—there it was the Maoris—and I had to come back

38

to Tahiti. I am Tahitian. I love Tahiti—the sun—the sea—the reef. Did you know they call me the Reef Girl?"

They had returned to the flower-bowered steps of the terrace, which was vacant. She turned to look up at him. "Are you like this with women always?" she asked. "You are very quiet. I have been talking and talking, while you . . ."

"Yes, I suppose I am—quiet I mean. But every one of these moments has been precious to me."

"Are you a poet?"

"No. But I do write."

"What do you write about?"

"Oh, about life as it might be. Romance, I suppose—in a world hopelessly realistic! Winifred says I'm out of step in this day and age."

"You could write very well, I think."

"Why do you think so?"

"I do not know. But you are not like other white men. You do not ask me to drink, or go to bed with you."

"Faaone, is that—so extraordinary?" queried Donald, startled by her frankness.

"It has never happened before, that I can remember."

"My God, what an opinion you must have of my race! But Faaone, there must be other white men who would not insult you. That Captain, the Frenchman who introduced me, surely—"

"He is a friend, a cousin of my mother's. He always has been kind. And he is a Frenchman, who are not like the English— But I did not mean I am insulted. How can I be when it is I who make them come to me? Yet—" She paused a moment, then went on. "Gossip makes me out a common whore. But I am not. I cannot be bought."

"Then what is it that—that makes you want to be the lover of white men, as I have heard?"

"It is hate!" There was such loathing in her voice that he

stepped back, aghast. She put her hand on his arm, as if to hold him. "But I do not hate you, Monsieur. I love you for what you did."

"Faaone, I—I don't understand you. What did I do?"

She gazed up at him with great midnight eyes. "You—you treated me as I have seen other white men treat the women they wish to honor. Perhaps it is because you are American. You seem to see that Tahitians have feelings. Even your sweetheart —she smiled at me. European women never do that, if they know who I am."

"Winifred is that way," replied Donald. "And you remind me that I must return to her."

"Monsieur, will you see me again?" she asked, as they halted at the steps. The moonlight played upon her alluring face.

Donald's heart gave a leap. "Faaone, would you like me to?"

"I have never asked any other white man anything."

"Then, yes. I will come to see you—or meet you," he rejoined, a little unsteadily. In the background, from beyond the moon-blanched garden and the dark slopes of the mountains, the voice of Tahiti seemed to call him.

"Not in town," she said quickly. "Your people—everybody— would think . . . My mother and I live out of Tautira, along the sea on the smaller island. We shall be home next week. Come out some morning early. I shall show you my reef."

"I'll come," he returned. And he led her round the terrace to her party, where he bowed his thanks.

Colonel Hendricks and his wife had left the table. Winifred, as he joined her and Mrs. Gannett, greeted him with dry good humor.

"Well, darling, you created a sensation. I hope you enjoyed it," she said. Her smile seemed guileless, but he could sense she was not as pleased as she made out.

"I'll say I did."

"So did I. But Bennet-Stokes certainly did not enjoy your conquest of Faaone. When you took her outside, he went into

40

a panic—wanted to follow you. He did, too, after I left him and came back to Mother."

"Don, she's lovely and, for all I could see, a lady," interposed Mrs. Gannett, brightly. "Since you wanted to dance with her, I liked the way you did it. After all, if you're going to write about Tahiti, you must meet the natives."

"Write? Mother, you're so naïve," interrupted Winifred acidly. "Don fell for the girl, hook, line, and sinker. Everyone saw that. His so-called gallantry didn't deceive me."

"Sure—I fell for her all right," retorted Donald, stung by Winifred's sudden change of manner. Impelled by a desire to strike back, he went on: "Who wouldn't? She's a bird of paradise. She's the finest dancer I ever led out on a floor. What's more, for all I could tell, she's as decent as anyone I ever met."

"You *did* get hit hard," snapped Winifred sarcastically. "But you can't expect us to swallow all that guff about how she's just like the girl next door—she's a tramp. Finish your drink, Mother. I want to go home."

"But I do not," protested Mrs. Gannett, with asperity. "This place is interesting to me. You two just stop looking daggers at each other."

Winifred, however, was not to be reproved. She had fire in her eyes. She finished her drink and then rose to leave, saying to her mother that she could stay with Donald if she liked.

"Dear me! What did you do to the girl?" complained the mother, getting up from the table. "I believe she's jealous of that beautiful savage."

"She is—and I'm delighted," said Donald as he led her out. "For once she's had a dose of her own medicine."

They quickly caught up with Winifred, who was quite capable of taking the car and driving off without them. No more was said. Donald tried to cool off during the ride home, with indifferent success.

It was a slow drive down the long dark lane from the main road to the cottage. Every foot of it held some marvel of tropic beauty—fantastic silver moonbeams, the song of the palms, the heavy fragrance of frangipani flowers, and the low melancholy roar of the reef—but Donald scarcely noticed. He helped the women out and then put the car away in its palm-thatched garage. When he returned to his cottage Winifred stood waiting for him, her fair hair shining in the silver light.

"Don, I want to talk to you," she said.

"I think you've talked enough. But if you want to fight—well, have at it!"

"I don't want to fight."

"That's one for the books—besides, I'm aching for one."

"What's the matter with you? You've never spoken to me or looked at me this way before."

"I never came to Tahiti with you before. You were at it again, making up to the likes of Bennet-Stokes, openly encouraging his advances! For God's sake, Win, why?"

"How can I tell what he is? Besides, what about you and Faaone? You—Donald Perth, the romantic—and a native whore!"

"She is not a whore!"

"Oh? Are you going to see her again?"

"She asked me to visit her in Tautira."

"And did you accept?"

"Yes."

There was a long silence. Finally Winifred looked up at him. Her deep violet eyes glistened—he could not tell whether from the moonlight, or unshed tears, or some passion he could not fathom.

"Don, I won't see Bennet-Stokes again, but you must not meet this native girl."

"Why not?" demanded Donald, still rebellious.

"She'd be fatal to any man, much less a romantic like you."

"All the more reason to see her. For in spite of all you say, I'm going to write romance—and be a success, too!"

"Ah, so that's it! I knew *something* had got to you. Don, once

42

and for all, why don't you give up this crazy notion of being a writer? I don't understand it and never will."

"I know—you've told me often enough. But I have a right to my one real ambition, and I won't give it up. Besides, I'm different down here—something I can't explain yet. It has to do with how I feel, not how I think. It's more natural, I guess. I used to have my emotions under control, for one thing. Now, all of a sudden, I'm jealous as hell about you even flirting with Bennet-Stokes."

At that her eyes softened and she answered him lovingly, "You really mean that, don't you darling? Perhaps Tahiti has changed you. But—you won't see that Faaone again, will you? Promise me—"

She put her arms around his neck and lifting her face kissed him passionately. With her fervor, his uneasiness at the sudden change in her mood melted away like mist before the sun, and he returned her caresses with interest. He promised not to see Faaone, and she agreed to marry him in June, shortly after their return home. After a while she coaxed him to walk along the shore under the moonlit palms.

When they returned, Winifred sat down in Donald's spacious hammock and drew him in with her. Together, they watched the ghostly moonbeams play on the surface of the lagoon, entranced by the unearthly beauty of the midnight hour.

Suddenly Donald was assailed by a heart-rending pang. He was not to see Faaone again, not to roam the beach with her, walk with her on a night like this under the tropic moon, hear her contralto voice, feel the magic of her touch. Never to know the mystery of her! He remembered her as she had been the moment she had asked him if he would see her again—the haunting light in her magnificent eyes, the thrill in her voice when she had said she loved him.

As if she sensed the direction of his thought, Winifred stirred beside him. Her arms went round his neck once more, and her lips sought his. He returned her embrace, at first almost me-

43

chanically, then more passionately, matching her ardor with his own. Restraint was not in her, and the movements of her hands and body had a rhythm that was one with the sigh of the wind in the palms and the hollow boom from the reef.

Suddenly her arms slid down from around his neck, and she slipped out of the hammock to her knees. There the moonlight caught her full in the face as she raised her head to look deep into his eyes. "Don," she whispered, "let's not wait." In a quick motion she slipped off her thin dress and stood up, her white-and-gold body bathed in the pale light. "Take me, take me— now!" she cried, holding out her arms.

But Donald did not move. He sat for a moment as if transfixed and then, with a shudder of revulsion, turned away.

"Donald, please— What's the matter with you?— Donald, *look* at me. Are you a man—or what are you?"

"I can't—I can't—it's just not right," was all he could muster, aware of a terrifying passion he could not fathom—a mixture of disgust and desire that had nothing to do with this girl he planned to marry. For, suddenly, it had seemed to him that Faaone stood before him, darkly beautiful, mysterious—seducer and destroyer of many such as he.

There was a long silence, broken only by the cry of some night creature far down the shore. Finally a small sound made him turn. Slowly, gracefully, Winifred bent to pick up her dress, her eyes glistening with tears and, at the same time, hardening as she gazed into his face. "Goodnight, Donald," was all she said as she turned and slowly, almost regally, walked down the porch steps and back to the main cottage.

Wordlessly, he stared at the white body receding in the moonlight, fading into the shadows near the house. He was conscious of shame, of terrible guilt. She would never forgive him for his failure. Nor could he ever tell her that it was not she who had repelled him but a vision of Faaone. God! He wanted her more than at any time he had ever known, but now it was too late. The picture of her, standing on the top step of the

44

porch, with the moonlight like a halo around her lovely face and form, was one he knew he would never forget. Never, anywhere, had Winifred been so beautiful as here on Tahiti. Surely this South Sea island held incalculable power over beauty, love, romance, and surely as well over evil and tragedy.

Acutely conscious of the specter of disaster that had haunted him since the beginning of the trip, he finally moved, stiffly, turning and walking down toward the beach. The moon had gone behind the towering peak of Orohena, and the silver radiance had darkened. Stars that had been dim began to blink again, and the Southern Cross, halfway to the zenith, stood out white and brilliant. But Donald walked up and down the beach, seeing nothing except, in his mind's eye, that exquisite white body, whose pale, fragile beauty seemed not to fit the tropic scene, and beside it the dark, voluptuous form of the beautiful Tahitian. It was nearly dawn when he returned at last to his cabin and fell, exhausted, into a restless sleep.

The next day, Winifred appeared much as she had always been—as gay and affectionate as if the previous night's events had never taken place. Donald felt a sense of relief, but his old nagging doubts and anxiety about what might happen in the future stayed with him.

5

❄

❄

❄

A week passed, and for the most part life resumed its former rhythms, with one important exception—Donald began to write.

The lovely Tahitian dawns had always entranced him. Several times he had tried to rouse Winifred to see the exquisite rose-colored clouds, too ethereal and evanescent to be true, and, just before the sun came up from behind the mountain, the glorious light of nameless color upon the water. But his appeals were in vain; if there was one habit that the tropics did not change in Winifred, it was her love of sleeping late in the morning.

The second dawn after the disastrous ball, Tahiti appeared as languorous as Winifred awakening from a tropic night, with sky-high columnar clouds of a rare rose gold hue rolling up over the mountain. And, seated on the ground under the flambuoyant tree on the point, Donald wrote the first words of his novel. It was the setting that inspired him. Whatever he made happen there would be true for him, and he began without constructive plot or even carefully thought-out characters. The moments flew by like magic. And so he discovered that Winifred's laziness was his good fortune; he could write while she slept. At last he felt the satisfaction of achievement.

As usual he joined Winifred, looking fresh and sweet in her white shorts and halter, and Mrs. Gannett for breakfast. He did not mention his writing.

"Don, darling, are you taking me places today?" Winifred asked.

"Places? Yes, Win, anywhere but to town."

"I'm tired of that. I want to go native."

"Go? You've gone, my love."

"What nonsense, Don!" spoke up Mrs. Gannett, over her cup. "To go native, as Mrs. Hasbrook explained to me only the other day, appears to be a sordid return to the animal. White *men* do it, she claimed, but only occasionally a woman. Ridiculous for you, Winifred. You're a lady of quality—a girl with position. The beachcomber state, as I understand it, would be impossible for you even in jest."

"I don't agree, Mother. It's natural and instinctive. It's what one *does* in Tahiti. Culture is only a veneer. Here you don't care for clothes or talk of books or work. You're just lulled into a dream of the senses. I adore it."

"Well, make the most of it, my dear. For even here time flies. We'll be going home soon."

Donald made no comment, though Winifred's words were surprisingly forceful. But he did not believe this South Sea enchantment would last long with her.

They spent the day wading for cowrie shells. Donald had to turn over the rocks and fragments because Winifred was afraid of crabs, spiders, moray eels, starfish, and many unknown creatures frightful to look at. Once a milk-hued eel darted between her bare legs, and she screamed.

"Darling, your desire to go native certainly doesn't extend to morays," he remarked.

47

"Uugh! I should say not. Anyway, it was a snake. Did you ever see so many queer animals? I never even dreamed of the lovely and ugly living things we see here."

"I did. Tahiti satisfies something in me—something I never knew was there."

The succeeding days were the happiest Donald had ever known, not excepting certain boyhood summers, of which they were reminiscent. His writing seemed to be a liberation of haunting voices that cried for expression. It somehow freed him of morbid thoughts and left him in the mood to play with Winifred. They passed the days, after breakfast, out in the open, wading, swimming, hunting, idling in the golden shade, paddling their outrigger canoe in rain and shine, making friends with the natives along the shore. Winifred sunburned to a lovely rich tan; if she needed more than that to perfect her beauty, she gained it in a little added fullness to her slender form.

Before long, however, Donald's book obsessed him, and the few hours from dawn till the late breakfast were not enough. He devoted himself to Winifred only until the midday siesta, after which he returned to his writing. Winifred complained about this, and once they quarreled. She accused him of neglecting her for Faaone, who was—she knew by now—to figure in the novel.

"Don, rumor has it that Faaone's first lover was her own father. Have you put *that* in your precious novel?"

"That's a lie!" cried Donald, furious, his eyes blazing.

"Look at you, Donald Perth! Did you ever burn like that for *me?* Anyway, it's not a lie. Catherine Bellair told me. She's been here for a long time, you know. And Mother's friend, Mrs. Hasbrook, told us the same thing. There must be something to it. That's why Faaone hates foreigners."

Donald had turned and walked away from her, leaving her standing on the porch. As he paced the beach, his fury abated. After all, people visiting Tahiti had nothing to do but talk. When he saw Winifred, he asked her not to speak to him again of Faaone. Perhaps sensing something in his tone, she did not take up the argument again, and her apology seemed to come from her heart.

At any rate, after that she apparently got over her feeling of neglect. She spent the afternoons up the beach with the villagers, either in or on the water, and she returned wet and disheveled, wholesomely tired and ravenously hungry. She babbled endlessly about the natives, especially the children to whom she grew attached, and about helping the fisherwomen draw their nets.

One sunset she came back, pale under her tan, her eyes dark with excitement, her scant raiment wet. Donald had never seen her more attractive.

"Oh, I've had the—most glorious time," she exclaimed, flouncing down to kick off her wet sneakers. "I've been out to the reef."

"What! With the northeast trade blowing and the tide so high? The surf has boomed like thunder all day. Are you crazy?"

"It was grand, Don. Tavarie and his brother took me in their big canoe. It was perfectly safe, believe me. Next time you must come with me. You haven't seen anything yet. . . . Once across the lagoon we got into the shoal water. I've never seen anything so beautiful as the coral, and the fish. On a calm day it would be simply glorious out there. They took me within a hundred feet of the outside of the reef, right up in the foam. We used to think there was surf on the Atlantic, but we never even *saw* a real wave. The big green combers were as high as this house, and when the spindrift blew off their crests, there were rainbows all along them. When a crest broke, it turned into a tumbling wall of pure white that crashed to ruin on the reef and raced across the coral ten feet deep, to spread all over, far out into the lagoon. The sun shining on the droplets of water was like the fire of diamonds. . . . Oh, Don, I'm sunk. I shall never be the same again!"

49

Donald was at first startled by her casual reference to Tavarie. How often had she seen the huge native since they had watched him lead the dance at the Bellairs' affair? But he could not help being caught up in her enthusiasm and agreed to go along the next day that there was a strong trade wind.

"You'll love it, Don. Come with me tomorrow. Tavarie's going to take me fishing for patia. We'll see the women fishing along the shore with their cane poles, too—and after dark the torches burning on the reef and the coconut-hull fires under the palms. It's all so different—so beautiful! It's another world, Don!"

Late the next afternoon Donald procured crude tackle, and he and Winifred paddled their outrigger to where Tavarie waited for them in his own canoe. The place he took them to turned out to be wonderfully glamorous. A succession of rollers thundered in from the long coral reef that extended far out. Huge swells rode out of the blue, rising and careening to curl and break and crash. There was a large area of water scarcely two feet deep where the smooth coral bottom was studded with coral heads—huge roses and thickets and grotesque pipe organs.

Tavarie smashed up crabs for chum, scattering it all over the shallow patch. "We wait," he said. "Patia come after dark."

The sun sank behind broken trade-wind clouds, the lower ones like sails on the horizon. It was a pearl and gold sunset, with vivid contrasts of purple. Clouds and sky were mirrored in the lagoon. Donald gazed spellbound at the wondrous spectacle and then turned to Winifred, to share with her the magic of it all.

She was smiling dreamily, but not at the sunset. Her dark gaze was on the giant native, whose half-naked body shone in the light. For a moment Donald was angry, but he said nothing, and his anger soon faded. After all, he reasoned, Tavarie is part of the scene. He could not wonder that the Tahitian, so like a pagan god, fascinated Winifred.

50

The lagoon became a dazzling blaze of orange and silver, with the reef, at low tide, a low black ragged line snowed under by every breaking wave. All of a sudden, as Donald had found happened in the tropics, the vivid life died out of the afterglow, and dusk—velvety, soft, darkening to bronze—confronted him. A full moon broke out of the clouds. The hour for patia fishing was at hand.

Tavarie strode to an edge of coral, and wading in a few feet, stood silhouetted black against the pale lagoon, his enormously long cane pole extended. As Donald watched, he gave a hard jerk. There was a splash, then the wrestling of a fish. Tavarie swung it in, removed the hook, and threw it on the beach, where Donald corralled it. Wiping the sand off, he found it to be about ten inches long, beautifully and powerfully built, bright silver all over, with a sharp nose and a broad tail. He dropped it in the empty bucket just as Tavarie pulled in another.

Winifred had imitated Tavarie, and suddenly she yelled for help. Turning, Donald saw that something was trying to pull the pole away from her. He ran to her assistance. The fun had begun.

"Hold your pole up, Win," he shouted. "There! Play him a little. Now, yank him out! There! You're a born fisherman, darling, and now you're on your own. I want to fish myself,"

Donald was no novice at fishing in salt water, and he was a keen angler. But, though he felt a hard strike and a run, he missed his first fish. He had not been prepared for its swift savagery. As he stepped back to put on another bait, he heard Winifred talking spiritedly to a fish that, evidently, she had not hooked. But before Donald got ready again, she had hooked another and got into difficulties.

"Save your pole, Win," he yelled, as using both hands she hauled the patia out on the shore. Then the fishing became fast and furious, so that Donald almost forgot to look at the huge white moon and listen to the surf. It was after midnight when the sport ended, and Donald paddled a sleepy Winifred back to the cottages.

Despite the delights of this expedition, however, Donald did not go again. It seemed that all he saw and felt in Tahiti, all that he dreamed might have been, added prodigiously to his book, and the longer it grew, the more fervidly he wrote. Increasingly, he left Winifred almost entirely to her own devices.

One morning in early May, three days before the northbound steamer was due, he finished his story. He called it *Faaone*. Now that it was finished, he laughed in sheer incredulity and exultation. He would mail it on steamer day. He was an author in his own secret pride, no matter how futile his efforts might prove.

He hurried across the hot open space between the cottages to Winifred's window. As he stepped up, the sweet intoxicating breath of frangipani blossoms assailed his nostrils. He brushed aside great clusters of double hibiscus bushes to look in at her window.

She was asleep in a sheer, pleated pink nightgown. She had forgotten to pull up the coverlet or had flung it aside. Her beauty struck Donald as always, but in this unconscious moment she seemed subtly changed. Her long, heavy lashes emphasized strikingly the faint blue shadows under them. Her beautiful face showed strain. About to call her gaily, for the breakfast hour was at hand, he stopped himself in concern. The girl, left to herself, had been playing too strenuously under the tropic sun. She looked tired, almost spent. Winifred never did anything by halves—of late, he recalled, she had been learning to dance the hula. Donald reproached himself. How delicate, exquisite, frail she was in her blonde loveliness!

At that moment, the tinkle of the breakfast bell disturbed her, and she stirred in her sleep. Her breast swelled with a long sigh. He called her. The golden head moved on the pillow, and her lids fluttered and opened to disclose wide eyes, dark with slumber. They quickened and her pupils dilated. Then she rolled over to hide her flushing face.

"Don!" she said sulkily. "What are you staring at?"

"I'm sorry, Win," he replied, a little taken aback. There seemed something aloof or alien about her. "I just finished my story. I wanted to tell you first."

"Congratulations, dear. You surely have slaved over it. What do you call it?"

"Faaone."

"I might have known! It's a good thing we're going home on the June boat—only a few weeks!"

"What do you mean by that? The book's not about the real Faaone. How could it be? I hardly know her and won't ever see her again. I used her name, that's all. Win, you strike me sort of odd. Don't you *want* to go home?"

"Oh, my God, yes!" she cried. "I've had enough of Tahiti. I wanted to go on this ship. But Mother wouldn't . . ."

The vehemence of this outburst surprised him. "Win, calm down, darling. You've been overdoing it all the time I've been working, I guess. I'm sorry—"

"It's not your fault, darling," she said more composedly. "Only it might have been better . . . Well, never mind. I'm okay —just too much sun. Tell Loo I'll have my breakfast in bed."

Donald got down and went thoughtfully around to the porch. He had breakfast with Mrs. Gannett, who, when he told her Winifred was not coming to join them, rather vehemently declared that he should not have allowed Winifred to run wild.

"As if *I* could have stopped her," he responded mildly. "What's this about Win wanting to go home on the May ship?"

"She did. I was dumbfounded. The other night she came home, I don't know how late, but late, and she looked so wild I was shocked. Her hair was down, all wet with dew and stuck full of frangipani blossoms. She'd been running among the flowers, she said. She was as white as a sheet and a sight to behold. It was then she asked me to take her home at once. But that's impossible. My new house will not be ready until the end of June. . . . Donald, I suggest that you take better care of

Winifred during the remainder of our stay."

Donald promised, but shortly went back to his final editing. He did not see Winifred until dinner, when she appeared radiantly beautiful again, if not quite her former gay self. The following day she was back in shorts, as usual.

After lunch on mail day, Donald drove Mrs. Gannett and Winifred to town. He left them chatting with acquaintances who came up and hurried toward the post office through the bustle and excitement incident to steamer day. For Donald there had always been a difference between the northbound and southbound steamer. But today's northbound ship was not only bound for home, it would be carrying his precious manuscript. Suppose it should be lost! He had not typed it, and had no copy.

The shady square and street in front of the big French post office were thronged with people, mostly natives. Donald stood on the lower step to gaze across the coral lagoon, the white crawling reef, the heaving blue sea, to Moorea, half-lost in pearl clouds. It would not be easy to leave Tahiti. Always afterward there would be something lost out of his life.

He was thinking about that, when a gentle hand touched his arm. He turned and his heart leaped. Faaone stood there, her other hand steadying a bicycle. Her small head, regal and dark, came up to his shoulder. She wore a rare white frangipani blossom over her left ear, which in native sentiment indicated that she was looking for a lover. White-gowned, slender, voluptuous, with magnificent jet-black eyes gazing into his—her beauty made Donald catch his breath.

"Faaone! You—I'm glad to see you," he stammered.

"Monsieur Donald, I have waited for you every morning." she replied.

"I'm sorry. Indeed I missed you more than you . . . I daresay you waited in the afternoon—or at night—for a luckier fellow," he returned lamely.

54

"I have not wanted to see any other man since that night at the ball."

"Faaone, I—I couldn't come."

"Ah! Your vahine—she did not want you to see Faaone."

"No, she didn't. You are wonderfully beautiful, you know. I didn't blame her."

"But, Monsieur, I did not want you to be like the others."

"I believe that, Faaone, but who else would? I couldn't—I didn't dare come. But I did want to—to see you on your reef."

"Donald, I will continue to wait for you."

"But we're leaving Tahiti next month."

Suddenly her expression, the tone of her voice changed. "You should have gone long ago, Donald. You kept *her* here too long."

"What do you mean?" he questioned sharply, alarmed by her intensity and the pitying, almost scornful, look in her eye.

"Haven't you heard the coconut radio?" she asked.

"No. What does it say?"

"Tahitians talk in riddles, Monsieur. The women tell of their love affairs with white men—proudly. The men brag and laugh. Lip by lip it runs."

"Well, what of it?" queried Donald, nonplussed. "What's that got to do with Winifred?"

"Tavarie brags, Donald."

"Tavarie!"

"Yes. About your lovely golden-haired vahine."

Donald quivered. Suddenly he had to fight to keep from striking her. But he could see she was not merely repeating gossip. She appeared profoundly moved.

"That's not true, Faaone," he said thickly. "Winifred hired Tavarie to paddle her around the lagoon—to teach her how to fish, and, you know, all the native tricks."

"Tavarie does not brag of that," rejoined Faaone. "Where a white woman is concerned, there is only one thing—love. Mon-

55

sieur Donald, you are an innocent boy—a trusting fool. But you are the only white man I ever respected. That is why I tell you. That is why I will wait for you out by my reef."

She turned and glided away, her beautiful braid of dark hair hanging below her waist. Donald stared after her, oblivious to the crowd, rooted to the spot, terribly, and for the moment irremediably, shocked.

6

A few minutes after his encounter with Faaone, Donald wandered from under the red canopy of flambuoyant trees out into the brilliant sunlight, blazing white and intense. The lagoon was a shimmering sheet of copper. Along the rock wall the water lay noiseless and green. Black-barred angelfish, with long streamers floating from their dorsal fins, nibbled at the vegetation on the coral. The air was thick with heat. An old bronze cannon, half-buried in the ground, was too hot for the touch of Donald's casual hand.

For weeks he had been living in a paradise of romantic expression, of susceptibility to ever-changing and unparalleled beauty, of self-fulfillment. He had been awakened rudely to reality, whether or not there was any foundation for Faaone's statements. In the same breath, almost, with which she had told him that she had waited for him every morning, that she did not want him to be like the others, that she would continue to wait until he came, she had repeated gossip so common that it had spread by the coconut radio. It was unbelievable to Donald, almost too monstrous to imagine. He had to ignore Faaone's frank words, to strive to forget the look in her eyes, to strangle

57

the arousal of base suspicion. Loyalty to Winifred and chivalry, no less than cool reason and intelligence, repudiated the gossip.

At length he made his way to the Cercle Bougainville, where, conspicuous in the colorful and humming café, he found Winifred and her mother with the Bellairs, Mrs. Hasbrook, and some American passengers off the ship. They were drinking and talking. Winifred, flushed of face, greeted him gayly.

"Don, dear, you look worn out—have a drink. Oh, the mail! What a stack of letters!"

Donald joined the group. "Decomposed is the word. I think it's a letdown after my work—and the sun."

Gradually, drink and lively conversation and some interesting news from the States relieved Donald's depression. The Bellairs were friendly and inquisitive about his book, about which Winifred had evidently told them. Bellair wore the same air of nonchalant and melancholy resignation as always. His handsome consort, fashionably gowned, brilliant and satiric, had a stimulating effect upon Winifred. In the background sat Bennet-Stokes, at a table with some officers from the ship. His face was red, and his hand shook as he lifted his glass. He returned Donald's look with a glassy stare.

In the succeeding two hours, most of the acquaintances Winifred and Donald had made in Tahiti, as well as the new ones of the day, drank and chatted and laughed with them. At length Winifred dragged Donald and her mother out of the café. "Don, you were a darling," she said, as they found their car. "Evidently writing improves your disposition. But, my dear, you can't hold your liquor. We'd better go home."

"Winifred, I'm not drunk," protested Donald.

"You will be pretty soon. Let's go."

Winifred insisted on driving, which was just as well, Donald thought. As they drove out of town, the sun was sinking behind the long western slant of Moorea, and a gorgeous panorama of mauve and saffron and salmon clouds lay banked in broken trade-wind procession along the horizon, silhouetted against the sky. A black sail crossed the golden vase-shaped sun as it slid behind the horizon.

As they disembarked from the car, Donald noticed that the back of Winifred's white silk blouse was wet with perspiration. And his garments, scant as they were, were also damp—one result of Papeete on a windless sultry day when drinks had been numerous. Don put on his bathing trunks and made for the lagoon. The exquisite sensation of cool water on his flesh after that blistering day was impossible to appreciate sufficiently. He had called Winifred to come, but she preferred a shower and reading her mail on her bed. Nor would she come outdoors with him later, though there was a moon rounding toward the full. Donald went to bed . . . weary in body and vaguely troubled in mind.

Next morning before sunrise, he was out, trying to recapture his joy in the dawn. He watched the vast concourse of rose-pearl clouds, majestically looming between him and the rising sun, breathed the ineffable fragrance of the early morning, and listened to the patter of the palms and the song of the sea. But his unease continued unabated.

Winifred did not get up until noon. She appeared the same languid and glamorous creature—yet not the same. Did the subtle indefinable difference exist only in his mind?

Now that Donald had finished his work, he was free to pursue the play on shore and lagoon. But that afternoon Winifred made excuses that were as transparent as crystal water. When she informed him she was going in to Papeete, he spoke sharp words that precipitated a quarrel.

"Darling, why don't you go see Faaone today?" Her tone was sarcastic. "You were seen talking with her yesterday. Quite a tableau the two of you made—oblivious to the gossipy world of Papeete. Why don't you keep your date with her?"

"I didn't make one."

"But she wanted you to?"

"Yes."

"Evidently you have made a conquest of Tahiti's most famous and beautiful whore!"

"If I have I'm not aware of it," he said, his face reddening with anger.

"Don, go play with Faaone. Perhaps you'll understand Tahiti better. I'll be seeing you—later." And she drove away with her mother, leaving Donald standing in the driveway, aghast and furious.

His first thought was that he *would* go to see Faaone. But he decided against that, sensing disastrous consequences for himself if he did. Her appeal was too tremendous to risk. Besides, he wanted to cherish the memory of Faaone, not as Tahiti knew her, but, in her beauty and her physical perfection, as the embodiment of his dream. Nevertheless all afternoon he had to fight the almost irresistible desire to go to her. More than anything he wanted to see her out on the reef. The Reef Girl! Somewhere he had heard that she was like a golden angelfish in the surf—that unlike most native women, she swam nude in the white breakers.

How bitterly Winifred had bitten out that speech! And scorn —why had she betrayed scorn in her mocking permission? Was she inviting him to fall prey to the physical and natural license of the native life? Her first wild response to Tahiti's demoralizing influence—that night she had importuned him to take her —was that behind her evident desire to throw him into Faaone's arms? Had she ever really forgiven him? He wished they were on the steamer that had sailed at dawn—on the way home, away from Tahiti's malevolent, seductive influence. Perhaps then the Winifred he had known might return.

About mid-afternoon he took a walk up the beach, but he could not look at the curling white reef without thinking of Faaone. Out there on that white foam, with its glints of green and blue, she would be Venus rising from the wave, the sum of all beauty that made men mad. He had renounced the lure, but

60

he could not obscure the picture in his mind. On his way back, he lingered to watch the native fishermen hauling their nets in the wide bay north of the point. The children flocked about him, and the natives were prodigal of smiles and greetings. Tavarie as usual was conspicuous, even among the other stalwart young giants, naked except for their pareus. Donald observed, in passing on, a new and pretty cottage beyond the cluster of thatched huts. His inquiry elicited the information that it was Tavarie's, along with a look he was hard put to interpret. The cottage had a porch that faced the lagoon. There was scarlet hibiscus against the background of golden bamboos and green palms. A low spreading flambuoyant tree gave a crimson glow to the air, and the ground was red with fallen blossoms. Donald had a queer sensation as he passed it, one that he did not care to analyze. He was aware of the dark inscrutable gaze bent upon him by Tavarie, and remembered the story about Tavarie's father, the Sweet-Scented Man, whose skull had been crushed by native lovers and husbands who had grown tired of his easy conquests of their women.

At dinner that evening Winifred apparently did not observe his mood. Her mail from home had at once upset and excited her. It appeared she had received bad news from her dressmaker and good news from someone whose name Donald did not catch, but which hardly offset the bad.

"I'll tell you what," she cried, suddenly radiant. "Let's stay here till the July boat."

"Winnie Gannett, you don't know your mind two days running," declared her mother.

"How about you, Don?"

"I don't want to leave," replied Donald. "But I wouldn't stay longer unless you married me."

"*Here?* Oh, you *are* funny," she burst out, with a gay laugh. "But you flatter me, darling."

"I don't see how."

"You meant I'd be an anchor—maybe I would. Probably I have been, for I know you've stayed away from Faaone, even today after that acid remark of mine."

"No, I did not avail myself of your gracious permission," he said a little distantly, with his eyes lowered. He changed the subject by announcing that he was going to town to see a prize fight, and invited her to go.

"Heavens no! These natives can't fight. Besides I want to read my mail again."

Donald recalled her opinion later, as he sat in the open air arena behind the big store. He watched three pairs of youngsters and as many grown men battle each other, and it was flagrantly plain that they could neither box nor stand pain. One good smack on the nose ended several of the bouts at once. The white men present laughed and egged on the combatants in vain. Such fighting, however, was not their real interest, and Donald reflected that when it came to paddling a canoe, or anything else to do with the sea, they were far superior to white men. He thought of the magnificent Tavarie, erect on the reef, his long harpoon aloft.

The fights, however, afforded Donald relief only while they lasted. Afterward, while standing under the light near the entrance, he saw Bennet-Stokes pass by, and his cold gaze was nothing if not derisive. It nettled Donald, and he decided he had had enough and went to find his car. The side street was crowded with Tahitians, talking and laughing in their low voices, and eating around the fruit vendors. On one street corner a throng of them was emerging from the motion picture theater, and gay laughter filled the flower-scented air. Donald had to stop his car at intervals to let the crowd split, and each time he was the recipient of bold dark glances from colorfully dressed women. He drove back to his cottage tired out and unsatisfied, his mind failing to shake oppression.

Next morning Donald again failed to enlist Winifred's enthusiasm for a jaunt on the beach or out in the lagoon. Wherefore he read and lounged on his porch. Winifred did not present herself for lunch, either, and Donald went back to his hammock and resorted to watching the Tahitians fishing on the reef through his marine glass. Tiring of that, he fell into a doze. When he awakened, Winifred was lying in the big hammock on the porch of her cottage. In a spirit of fun he looked at her through his glass.

She appeared far from asleep, but she certainly was oblivious to Donald's scrutiny. Over her face she held a sprig of frangipani, with a number of blossoms, and she was evidently enjoying their perfume. She was rolling gently from side to side. When the frangipani flowers fell away and her face was exposed, she looked lovely and dreamful in the extreme. Her eyes were closed, and her breast rose and fell too quickly for composure. Her expression was that of a girl in the throes of intoxicated love, and her slender form had a sinuous cat-like grace suggestive of supple power.

As long as Donald had known Winifred, he had never seen her exactly like this. It was as if the exotic fragrance of the frangipani blossoms had permeated to the very core of her. He was singularly, curiously affronted. It was a common gesture for foreign visitors on Tahiti to smell flowers, especially the frangipani and the faint, jasmine-like tiare-tahiti. But this prostration of Winifred's was different. All this world of sea and coral, of gold and green, of fragrance and languor, burned upon by the blasting sun, evidently worked incalculably upon her senses. She was a white woman under the sun of the tropics, and she should not have been there.

It required an effort to direct his attention elsewhere and throw off the insidious variations of gloomy thought. Until dinnertime, he walked to and fro on the beach. Always that relieved his agitation by forcing upon his mind sensations from without. The blessings of Tahiti were all physical.

At dinner Winifred did not appear to notice his abstraction. "Will you walk along the beach?" he asked, after Mrs. Gannett

63

had left the table. "It will be a full moon night."

"But not till late. I'm too tired to stay up," she replied.

Donald strove to make her growing aloofness nothing to worry about and to put himself in her place. Tahiti was superlative, but if one were not active outdoors, or did not drink indoors, or have a powerful incentive such as his writing had been, its subtle and indefinable moods worked upon white people. To let oneself go—to let go of all that education, custom, reason, had prescribed—that was the supreme urge in this sunny isle of gold, set in its azure pearl-reefed sea. "Go! Go where?" muttered Donald. "Not native—not Win!"

At nine o'clock Donald found himself undressing in the dark on the little sleeping porch of his cottage. To go to bed so early was a mistake for him. After six hours or thereabouts, he would have his sleep out and awaken to become prey to the night, the unknown—he and the natives had at least one thing in common and that was their fear of the dark. Nevertheless, he lay down. For a while he watched the white fire of the stars in the intense blue, and then he fell asleep.

He awoke with a start. The night was as bright as the sun-flooded day, only unreal and appallingly lovely. He became conscious of an oppression—this was, he knew, merely the bearing down of the tropics upon vitality at its lowest ebb, but it felt like a heavy weight upon his chest. He lay there quietly, his mind leaping to thought. What had awakened him? The answer was not the moonlight or the silken patter of the palms or the mournful drum of the surf. If he had awakened from a bad dream, as happened to him at times, he could not recall a vestige of it. Nor had he had his sleep out! In the moonlight, he could not see the radium hands on his watch and had to put it under the coverlet to make out the time. It was exactly midnight. He had slept only three hours. Yet here he was vividly awake. Whatever had pierced his slumbers must have been something spiritual or occult, surely the work of his subconscious mind.

64

But as he sat up in bed, he saw a slender dark form glide along the hibiscus hedge. It was that of a girl, and not a native. When she emerged from the shadow, the moon shone like burnished silver on her small head.

"Winifred!" whispered Donald. Something as strange as his awakening inhibited his impulse to call. She was not simply sauntering along, reveling in the beauty of the night. She was not dreamily watching the moon or listening to the song of the reef. She glided along swiftly, erect, straight into the palm grove, headed across the point.

Donald began to shake. What was she up to? Slipping into his sneakers and pants, he stepped off the porch to follow her. The moonlight was so bright that he could see her even under the shadow of the palms. When he ascertained that she was deliberately keeping to the denser patches of shade, he knew! This meant a rendezvous with Tavarie! His leaping conviction, like a fire along his nerves, burned away his hesitation.

"So help—me—God!" He strangled the cry in his throat. "Faaone did not lie!" In the agony of that whisper was the blasting of faith, of love that had been born in boyhood.

Winifred continued on, sure-footed and swift. Fear was not in her, nor doubt. Her goal was a magnet. She was a wild creature, seeking adventure, romance. Somewhere in the moonlit grove Tavarie would be waiting. They would walk under the palms along the beach, Donald thought, perhaps go for a moonlight canoe ride on the lagoon. There were no words to describe the enchantment of the midnight hour. It was unearthly lovely. Perhaps she could not be blamed for succumbing to that—for weaving a romance around a young Tahitian giant, for seeing in him one of the gods of old primitive legend. But Winifred, if she had thought at all, must know the native could not help loving her.

Gaining on her, Donald slowed his unsteady pace. Still she never looked back. All behind her must have been forgotten. Again she crossed a small open glade where the moonlight silver-fired her hair. How lithe, free-striding, beautiful she was! The palm leaves rustled softly; the boom of the reef grew louder, like low thunder in the distance; the fragrance of frangipani wafted intoxicatingly down the aisles of the palms. The moon, enormous and round, white as sea foam in the sun, and surrounded by a vast silver green luster, soared magnificently above the black slope of the mountain. Somewhere a brook murmured over stones on its way to the lagoon. No voice, no human sound, broke the spell. All Tahitians—except, no doubt, the son of the Sweet-Smelling Man—lay sound asleep in their huts.

Watching and pursuing like a savage, Donald's senses recorded every sight and sound and smell, every stimulus thrust upon his sensitive mind, flayed raw. This supernatural loveliness must be the reason for Winifred's aberration—every detail of it would be impressed on Donald's memory forever. Ever afterward, he thought, he must hate the moonlight.

Presently she would meet Tavarie on the beach. What then? Donald resolved to confront them. He would curse the Tahitian, frighten him as a white man could any native, and he would give Winifred the hardest few moments of her life.

But Winifred did not meet Tavarie on the beach. She kept on, crossing the wide point to the shore of the bay beyond. She did not hesitate. She did not look around, as a woman might who expected a lover. She kept to the edge of the grove, on and on, round the curve of the bay, on toward the scattered huts of the village.

Donald gained the shoreline. The coconut palms spread a fringe of shade along the coral sand. Across the width of the moon-blanched bay, Tavarie's new palm-thatched cottage shone like a pearl in the shadows. Only then did Donald realize that his sweetheart, his promised wife, the daughter of a New England family, was on her way to meet the Tahitian in his hut!

He saw her vanish in the doorway, dark against the thatched moonlit wall. Uncertainty ceased, and he fell upon his knees, with eyes fixed upon that door. Even now, he tried to force from his mind what he knew must be true. Winifred should—surely she would—come out immediately. She only wanted Tavarie to walk with her, to paddle her around the lagoon.

But she did not come. Donald was close enough to see the red shine of the flambuoyant blossoms in the moonlight, to smell the frangipani tree. The silence, broken only by a whisper of leaves, by the soft lap of waves on the sand, fell upon him like a weighted mantle. Throes of a horrible nightmare! But no! At that instant a flower fell upon his hand, a blossom from the wild hibiscus tree against which he leaned. Faaone's magnificent eyes, dark with scorn, darker yet with pity, burned in his memory.

Donald felt himself forced to his feet, as if by a fiery hand upon his quivering heart. Nostrils and lips expanded to draw in deep breaths. He stood there a moment, horror yielding to fury. He must *know;* he must *see.* With prodigious bounds he made for the cottage.

As he looked in the door he heard a soft sound. The room was dark, but a broad beam of moonlight poured through a window, and rays of brightness penetrated the slits between the bamboo poles that formed the walls. Tavarie, a gigantic figure, stood erect, like a listening statue. On the bed, dark against the white spread, lay Winifred's slight form.

Stepping inside, Donald called her name. The pulsing drum-thunder in his head muffled his voice to his own ears, but Tavarie spun around, and the girl cried out as she rose and then with arms upflung fell backward. Like a tiger Donald leaped upon the Tahitian to clutch his throat in hands of steel.

As his fingers buried themselves in tightening, convulsive flesh, a fiendish ecstasy, hot and gushing, washed over him. To tear open this brawny neck! He yielded to an incalculable yet somehow familiar power—savage, inexorable, beastly—that burst from him through his clenched hands.

But he was no match for the giant Tahitian. Tavarie lifted and

67

flung Donald from him. Crashing backward through the bamboo framework of the door, he went hurtling to the sand. Tavarie followed, looming over his attacker. His huge bare foot shot out. Donald swerved, but the kick struck his shoulder with savage force, knocking him flat. He heard a rumble from Tavarie's broad chest and his own hard panting. As he raised himself to his elbows, the giant launched into a leap. Donald nimbly rolled aside so that the great flat feet thudded into the sand. Bounding up, he snatched a green coconut and swung it with all his might. It cracked on Tavarie's skull and caromed high. The Tahitian went down heavily.

Donald leaped to strangle him once more. But instinct and cunning prevailed. He must not get too close. His lightning-swift glance swept the sand for a weapon. A rock, a club—to brain this bronze-hued, naked giant! Suddenly his eyes fell on Tavarie's long-poled harpoon tipped with single-barbed iron. With that in his hand he would have the magnified strength of devils!

"Goddam you—I'll kill you. . . . You sweet-smelling bastard!" Almost sobbing with rage, he seized the harpoon, and his eyes glued themselves to the rising native. This Polynesian giant—a god to brown women, fatal to the white—this hulk of putrid, mindless flesh and bone—it should rot and stink in the sand. The huge form, with its head like a horned demon's, its eyes of green fire, fangs of white, again launched itself into the air.

Donald eluded the brawny arms and with a tremendous thrust plunged the harpoon through Tavarie's middle. Impaled on the heavy iron, the man screamed, awakening the silent shore and galvanizing in Donald all that was primitive and ferocious. He cursed the giant. He laughed at the futile beating of his hands upon the harpoon shaft and gave the pole a dragging wrench. To pull the spear out, to ram it through that shining body again! The iron came out halfway, then caught on a bone and stuck. Donald shoved it back and through, clear to the shaft. Something wet and hot ran down upon his vise-tight hands. Blood! He felt it, smelled it, and reveled in his triumph.

The giant began to weave and totter across the sand, with the harpoon shaft describing half circles, quivering like an aspen leaf. Death loomed on his ghastly features as he staggered along the shore silhouetted against the moonlit sky, the harpoon extended at right angles from his abdomen.

For moments Donald saw only the struggling giant spitted upon his own spear, tearing out his insides with his wrestling. But then he heard the shrieks of women and the hoarse shouts of men swelling above Tavarie's screams, and they brought him to his senses. Villagers, some white-gowned, others naked save for pareus, ran down the shore, uttering discordant and haunting cries. When Tavarie plunged down like a gored bull, they surrounded him with shrill and fatalistic lamentations.

Donald ran back into the cottage. Winifred lay where she had fainted, her dark robe opened to reveal the pearl white of her rounded breasts. He took her in his arms and carried her out the back door, into the shadows of the palms. He had no sense of her weight and strode swiftly, not looking back. The melancholy cries began to grow faint.

As he crossed a moon-silvered glade, he wrenched his gaze to the girl in his arms. She appeared as fair as an angel. No havoc on that lovely face, with its dark, downcast lashes on waxen cheeks. Then her eyes opened and for a fleeting instant they were strained bottomless gulfs looking into his. They set blankly and rolled back under white lids.

"Help me, God!" Donald's voiceless cry rose up to the silent stars. They shone down pitiless, aloof, immutable. There was no help. The world of whispering palms and moonlit aisles mocked him. Rats ran down the marble boles of the trees—rats that sneaked out in the night! The surge on the reef pounded in deep detonations. He felt raindrops on his face. A black cloud, swooping out of the north, silver-rimmed and trailing long veils of gray, would soon hide the moon.

Donald hurried on, his mind still working, despite the emo-

69

tions that racked him. Reaching the cottages he noiselessly carried Winifred up the steps and into her room, where he laid her down on her rumpled bed. She appeared to be stirring back to consciousness. The silk robe, falling apart once more, revealed her nude—pearl, and gold-hued—in the soft light.

Her nakedness would damn her to dishonor. At any minute now she might be found out. "Winifred," he whispered and shook her, not gently. Indeed he clutched her shoulder brutally. Again she stirred, this time with a faint moan, but she did not revive. Donald's eyes searched the room until they rested upon her nightgown, crumpled into a silken ball, half-hidden under her pillow. He shook it out. Then, roughly, he pulled the robe from her arms and shoulders. He was not blind, but he could have prayed to be so, for this grace, this contour, and softness now could never be his. He slipped her into the silken nightgown and tied the ribbons with shaking hands. Then he pulled the dressing gown back around her. That done, he covered her, and with an air of finality rose to his feet.

His first thought was to arouse Mrs. Gannett and the servants, but he put that idea from his mind quickly. Her mother, the servants, the neighbors, the police, must not know. He may have been seen by the villagers, but who would know that Winifred had been there? If only she had not visited Tavarie before! He tried to push that maddening thought from his mind as he went slowly back along the moon-drenched walk to his cabin.

Then, suddenly, the enormity of what he had done struck him. He really was not a primitive hero rallying to the rescue of his mate, but a common murderer. Tavarie had taught him to fish for patia and could not have helped loving Winifred. There was blood on his hands, and it was not figurative but real.

As the conflict within him raged, bitter and unyielding, he cursed Tahiti, its unparalleled splendor, its debilitating heat and oppressiveness. It had led him, as it had many before him, to dishonor and ruin. Now, somehow, he must flee—get away from everyone and from the terrible guilt that was overwhelming him. When he reached his cabin, he slowly dressed himself as if in a daze and then paused to pick up his car keys. He remembered that at the southeast end of Tahiti there was a primitive wilderness, where the reef and road ended in a succession of steep cliffs and crashing surfs. There, perhaps, he could hide.

He drove along the winding road, oblivious of everything but the narrow ribbon of light ahead enclosed by the headlights of his car, past Papaenoo, toward Taravao. At the isthmus he turned toward Vairao on the smaller island. Beyond Taravao, the road was very narrow and full of chuckholes, but at this hour there was no other traffic. He had never been on this stretch before, but he knew that it would eventually end, and that would be his starting point.

Burned indelibly into his mind, as if with a searing iron, was the image of Winifred half-naked on that bed with the Tahitian towering over her. But there were other thoughts as well. There would be an investigation and a hearing. Possibly, no one had seen him clearly in his battle with Tavarie. But they would have seen a white man, and his running away would surely lead the authorities to charge him with Tavarie's murder. If he gave himself up or if they found him, he would probably spend the rest of his days in a stinking French jail or face the guillotine. In his numbed state, this prospect did not terrify him. Life was at an end anyway. But he could never go back to *face* them. He would kill himself first, perhaps by jumping off one of those great cliffs at the end of the island. Perhaps that would be the best way out—to end all his torment in the fathomless, forgiving sea.

The road became narrower and narrower until it was virtually no more than a two lane trail, and finally it ended altogether at the bank of a placid stream, which meandered down from the north to the sea. Donald turned the car around and drove back until he found a fairly level spot enclosed with a cover of thick jungle brush. Without hesitation, he plunged the car into the

71

brush, and was able to make about thirty yards before running off into a swampy area. Walking back to the road, he noted with grim satisfaction that when he had brushed away the tire tracks, no vestige of the car could be seen.

He turned back across the stream. The fairly well-marked trail could be seen easily in the bright moonlight. As he walked along slowly, the boom of the surf on the reef gradually became louder. Eventually the trail left the flat and moved up among the dark trees, toward the black mountain silhouetted dimly in the stars. It grew steeper and narrower as it wound back and forth up the steep slope. Finally, as Donald came up out of the dense trees into smaller brush, he could see the white edge of the reef glistening in the moonlight, where it curved toward the black cliffs.

"Land's end," he muttered. The end too, he thought, of all his hopes, his joys, his dreams—shattered beyond redemption in that one terrible moment. He was no longer Donald Perth, writer, dreamer, romanticist, but Donald Perth, murderer, outcast, and fugitive!

As he worked his way up the steep slope, he saw the faint white glow of dawn peeping out over the dark and heaving sea. He felt calmer now, though from a numbness rather than a resolution of his conflict. As the first pale red fingers appeared on the horizon, he reached the top of the ridge and went down into a tiny valley, which meandered out toward the end of the island. In a few minutes he had reached the end of the trail— the steep black cliff that plunged precipitously down into the dark gray sea. On either side of him, the sheer mossy cliffs stretched as far as he could see. Here at last was the end of the world. As an ironic complement, here also was a Tahitian sunrise bursting upon him with all its incomparable glory. In that moment of splendor, his own dark thoughts were briefly forgotten.

Straight ahead of him, a massive cumulous cloud towered thirty thousand feet into the air, its bottom streaked with gray veils through which some red light shone, its center an opalescent pink and red, its top burnished gold. The rays of the rising sun cast a shimmering red path from the horizon, clear up to the base of the cliff. A quarter of a mile from shore the sunken reef shallowed, and the huge waves, spawned by the trade winds thousands of miles away, rose ponderously, to turn green, crest and break, and become deep blue again before finally crashing against the face of the cliff. The scene suddenly took Donald back to his boyhood, when he had stood on the hills overlooking the sea near his home in Massachusetts and wished he could ride that red-gold track out past the limitless horizon.

But more recent memories soon returned. For a considerable time, he stood there wondering whether he should make that one step out into the dark waters that would close around him eternally. He thought of Winifred and her many moods and her startling beauty. His mind went over again those terrible moments at Tavarie's cottage. But, even as he urged himself to jump, something held him back. Somewhere along the lonely edge of these cliffs would be a beach with a few trees and some water. There, living as the natives did on breadfruits and coconuts, perhaps he could find himself again and gather the courage to go back and try to make amends for his terrible deed.

He stared up at the mountains to the north. They were steep, with many knife-like ridges running down toward the cliffs, and covered with short, wiry underbrush, but they appeared to be passable to the climber. Perhaps around and over the high cliff would be the beach that he sought.

The sun gradually moved up into the sky as Donald commenced his laborious ascent. Before long, the realities of his predicament began to overtake him. He had not brought a hat or made any provision for food or water, and he was soon scorched, tired, and scratched from his many encounters with the brush. But he continued on grimly, over what seemed like never-ending ridges. By the time afternoon had come, he was exhausted and parched. Though he could see an endless succession of rain squalls borne by the winds that thrust against the higher mountains of the island, none passed close enough to relieve the heat or his thirst. Finally, in one of the deeper valleys between the ridges, he found a tiny trickle of spring water and decided to spend the night there before trying to move on.

That evening he lay on his back on a grassy hummock, gazing up at the myriad of stars, the Southern Cross glistening like a bright jeweled diadem set in their midst. His torment had lessened, but his thoughts were bitter and melancholy. For a long time he had not thought of Faaone, but she came vividly to mind now. She had said that, of all the white men she had known, she trusted and respected him most. That would be over now. She would hate him for killing Tavarie, as would all the natives. He had lost her; he had lost Winifred; he had lost everything. Why had he not chosen that moment at dawn on the cliff to make a final, bitter end? But despite his despair, the possibility of suicide seemed to be irrevocably behind him. Finally, wearied by his endless recriminations, he fell into a troubled sleep.

The next morning found him climbing the steep ridges once again, struggling to worm his way through the endless brush, whose spiny arms thrust at him savagely as he crawled in and around, up and over them. Ultimately he reached the top of the higher ridge and worked his way down through the little valley, where he could again see past the point of coastline. He was dismayed to discover that as far as he could see there was the same starkness of plunging cliffs, with no beaches to be seen anywhere. The spiny ridges to the north ended in a sheer lava face, with a plunge of a thousand feet or more down into the ocean. Perhaps the golden beach he had heard about was a myth, and there were only these endless cliffs, winding clear back to Tautira in the north. There seemed no other way out than to try to climb over the top of the two-thousand-foot mountain—or to retrace his steps. But he could not go back.

Then he noticed that the trade wind, which had been at his face when he started his long climb, was now behind him, and he had an idea. Although the wind-driven swells were huge, they did not curl over and slap against the shore as on the reef, but pushed up ponderously against the cliff walls. This was deep water, and Donald was a strong swimmer. Perhaps he could swim to the beach, if one existed. If not, maybe he could find an opening in the reef somewhere on the north side of the island. He knew that there would be no turning back once he had plunged into the water. But it would be better to die in the sea this way than on a French guillotine.

He worked his way down to the lowest point of land, about thirty feet above the waves. When he reached it, he took off his shoes and tied them around his neck. Then, timing a wave as it came in, he plunged into the ocean. The backwash pushed him some distance away from the cliffs before he came to the surface. The thought of sharks crossed his mind as he swam slowly to the north towards the jutting promontory, about a mile away. But there had been few known attacks on swimmers by sharks at Tahiti, and, anyway, it was too late now to worry about them.

Though the morning wind was still light, the swells were high, and it was not easy to maintain his distance from the fatal cliffs. He swam slowly, pausing to rest frequently, but by the time he reached the cape he was tiring. To his dismay he saw only another deep cove and still another point a half mile away. He had almost reached the limit of his endurance when he rounded it and found ahead of him the black sand beach he sought. It curved around the cliffs to where the reef began again, with a grove of coconut palms on its fringe. Behind it was a valley into which a lacy waterfall streamed down from the green brooks above. There was an old hut at the edge of the trees. Donald struggled on, becoming wearier with every stroke. Finally, with a burst of second wind he brought himself almost within range of the beach.

Here was another peril—the huge waves that crashed incessantly onto the steep beach. They broke so close to the edge of the shore that it would be impossible to dive under them and reach land between the breaks. He must somehow try to ride through them and hope for the best. He thought it wiser to stay near the top of the nearest wave, on the outside, and swim as hard as he could before the next one overtook him. When he reached the breakers, his timing seemed perfect. He rose up on the top of a wave that broke ahead of him and swam with all his remaining strength. But the second wave loomed over him and crashed upon him with a fury that rolled him over and over, smashing him relentlessly against the rocky beach. As it receded, he tried to claw his way up, but his strength was gone and he began sliding back. A second wave smashed at him, and a third. He had lost all track of time and space when he vaguely heard shouts and saw two almost naked men running towards him on the beach. He felt strong arms reaching out to him, pulling him out of the surf and dragging him up to a safe place. He was conscious of them rolling him over and standing over him, before his senses wavered and he slid off into oblivion.

7

❋

❋

❋

Donald awoke not knowing for a moment where he was or how he got there. But his senses gradually cleared enough for him to appreciate the magnificence of his surroundings and to notice the three naked white men sprawled on the sand in the shade of the palms.

One of the three, a man of Herculean build wearing only a strip of pareu round his loins, arose at his call.

"Good morning, brother." His smile was friendly. "You ought to be dead, but except for a few bruises you seem to be all right. Where did you come from?"

"I climbed up over the mountains—that way." Donald sat up and pointed toward the south. "When I couldn't climb any more, I swam. But who are you?"

The man laughed in his booming way. "Well then, that's a good question. They call us 'nature men.' The natives think we're crazy. Perhaps you could call us refugees from civilization. So you came over the cliffs! That is something! I don't believe anyone has ever done it before."

Turning, he gestured to his companions. "Meet my associates

—Monsieur Deverie and Monsieur Mathie. And what is your name?"

"Donald—Donald Smith."

"American, I take it. Well, we're glad you came to visit us." He gave no sign that he had noticed Donald's reluctance to give his last name.

Donald remembered hearing rumors of white men who had renounced civilization and gone to live as natives on the extreme east end of Tahiti—rumors which many had discounted, but which apparently were true.

The other two men greeted Donald simultaneously, verbosely and with exuberant enthusiasm. Monsieur Deverie was a little man with piercing, dark eyes, a sallow skin, and scant beard. He was naked and sunburned black. Monsieur Mathie, also stark naked, had hair of wondrous length and golden hue. He wore it pulled over his shoulder in a great stream, so that it spread and covered his torso, reaching nearly to his knees. The effect was startling; if he had not been presented as a male, Donald would have taken him for a woman, and a beautiful one.

"I'm English, name of Caldwell," boomed the giant. "You're welcome, Smith, whether curiosity or chance or God sent you to us. Whatever it was, you will profit by a sojourn here. And if you become one of us you will be free and happy, one of nature's sons."

They helped Donald up and led him back under the palms to a sandy-floored, palm-roofed shelter, behind which stood a couple of thatched huts. The place was strikingly clean. Oranges, bananas, breadfruits, mangoes, papayas, coconuts, lay on fresh-laced matting. There were no chairs.

Donald's head ached, but it began to function—especially after Caldwell graciously came up with a bottle of wine, and he had a drink. Monsieur Deverie built a little fire on some flat stones. Monsieur Mathie, presenting an astonishing figure as he stalked off to the beach, waded into the water, where there was a little corral made of bamboo sticks. He procured a live fish and

78

fetched it back wriggling in his hand, spitted it without cleaning, and roasted it over the fire. There was no salt, no bread, no sugar—nothing but fruit and the bottle of wine and the one fish for Donald.

"Usually we eat our fish raw," said Caldwell, making conversation. "We never have fires, except for guests, who come but seldom. Once a year Monsieur Mathie's sweetheart comes all the way from France."

"What do you do here besides gather fruit and catch fish?" queried Donald.

"That doesn't take long. Half an hour every other day. The rest of the time we do nothing."

"Nothing?"

"We rest, and invite our souls. We are away from the sordid, mad, ignorant world. Free!"

Donald said to himself that these men were crazy. But then, what about himself? After all, he was here with them, wasn't he?

"I see what you're thinking," declared the giant, with a huge smile. He made circular motions with his finger, pointing at his head. "Same as the natives. You think we've got wheels in our heads. That is quite wrong. The natives have nothing in their heads, and it is the world which has wheels. Listen, brother— I'm a nature man. I've lived here nine years, and I'm not a day older. I've had no money, no work, no trouble, no illness, no selfishness, no hate, no love, during all that time."

"But, man," expostulated Donald, nettled, "aren't you wasting your life?"

"No. I'm living it gloriously."

"You have no ambition?"

"None."

"You're not doing anyone any good."

"No, unless to do no one harm is to do good."

"Do you read?" asked Donald.

"But seldom. Newspapers are full of politics, war, class ha-

tred, murder, divorce, nations intriguing against each other—
so much that is false. The magazines are almost as bad. If we
could get good books, we'd read them. I find, however, that it's
better not to read anything."

Donald gazed about him. The place was the most profoundly
beautiful he had ever seen. Back behind the beach, a crystal
stream poured down over mossy rocks from an amber-shad-
owed tunnel of tree foliage. A cliff abutted the far side, and it
might have been painted, so colorful and figured did it appear.
From its top waved lacy ferns and long silver plumes, which
enticed the gaze upward to a magnificent mountain slope, the
summit of which was lost in clouds as white as snow. No blue
sky showed on that side, but there was a hint of blue through
the rifts in the foliage above the stream.

The western end of the sandy beach curved gracefully and
disappeared in a wall of green. Evidently the mountain
dropped sheer at that point. Back of the beach, the sand bench
rose gradually for a few feet, to run level for a hundred yards,
and terminate in terrace after terrace of ferns and flowers and
foliage, intricately mixed. There were scores of coconut palms,
leaning toward the sea, their long graceful leaves waving or
drooping or fluttering in the soft breeze. More golden leaves
than green took the intense sunlight.

Offshore, perhaps a mile to the west yet seemingly closer, lay
an island, surely the gem of all Tahiti's numerous isles. Perhaps
a few acres in extent, with its stately grove of palms surrounded
by a beach of lucent sand, it was protected in front by a jagged
reef of black coral, against which a second surf curved in, to roll
and break melodiously.

Donald wondered if the nature men felt anything besides
their freedom. Apparently they paid no attention to their environment. For while he had been drinking in the beauty all
around, they had been absorbed in a most heated argument.
They kept talking, gesticulating. Finally Donald stretched out
and fell asleep.

80

When he awakened the sun had passed on over the mountain, so that, though still high in the sky, it had left this eastern point in shade. Blue lights trailed across the lagoon; blue tints touched the snow of the surf; blue spindrifts floated from the crests of the outer barrier.

"I tell you, Macnish would have died in any event," Caldwell was saying. His companions vociferously exclaimed against this.

Donald sat up to listen. They talked and argued. Back and forth they rocked on their brown haunches. The Frenchmen were intensely in earnest. The Englishman was loud and emphatic, but he did not give way to excitement. His argument seemed to be that a nature man should not try to subsist solely upon a diet of coconuts.

During the ensuing hour, which saw the approach of sunset, Donald pieced together what it was all about.

Macnish, a Scotsman, a nature man and a friend of Caldwell's, had come to Tahiti from Samoa some years before. He joined the colony on the east end and began experimenting with the variety and amount of his food. Despite Caldwell's advice he first gave up fish, which like the others he ate raw, and then one fruit after another, until only bananas, breadfruits, and coconuts remained. At this juncture, he had embarked on a trading schooner for the Fijis, where, having reduced his diet to coconuts alone, he died.

Evidently Caldwell did not dominate or convince his comrades, but he had more endurance and he tired them out.

"Brothers, you've had this conviction ever since news of poor Macnish's death came. And all my arguments leave you unconvinced. A diet of coconut milk and fruits will suffice for a shipwrecked sailor, for which use God evidently intended it, or for any man for a limited time. But, if he persists in that diet, he will eventually starve to death."

"It would be best not to eat anything," replied Mathie. "Nature did not intend us to live on flesh. Therefore I don't see why fruit, and one kind of fruit, is not enough."

"My brother, *you* eat cooked meat and drink wine when Mademoiselle Jeanette comes to visit you here," rejoined Caldwell. The golden-haired Frenchman seemed to have no ready answer for that. He sprawled surlily on the sand. Donald watched them unobtrusively. If he had been himself he would have been tremendously interested. As it was, he wondered what he had got into.

"What the hell have they got that I haven't—or didn't have before?" he muttered, as he went off toward the beach at the base of the cliffs, from which long windfalls tumbled down into the sea. Certainly this was not the solitude he had sought. But the nature men seemed to have no real interest in who he was or why he was there. Perhaps it was better, after all.

Shells had been a passion with him. Here there were many —cowries, clams, spirals, and others he could not name. Apparently the nature men did not care for shells. Did they love beauty? Was it love of beauty, longing for solitude, passion for the freedom they raved about, that nailed them to this martyrdom?

From the west end of the beach he watched Mathie out on the lagoon in an old canoe with a patched sail rigged clumsily on its mast. The Frenchman sat in the stern, steering with the paddle, his hair shining gold in the sunlight. He made a picture not to forget.

Donald collected a hatful of shells and returned to his palm tree to lay them in the sand. He asked Caldwell where he should sleep.

"Sleep?" asked the giant. "Wherever you want. But there's a bed of moss and a mat in the hut."

"How about mosquitoes?"

Caldwell emitted a laugh. "They never bite us."

"But they'll bite me."

"Undoubtedly. But when your skin is tanned, as God intended it to be, mosquitoes will no longer try to suck your blood."

82

"How about fleas, scorpions, rats?"

"None here."

"Do natives ever get out this far?"

"But seldom."

"Any women?"

"No. They are afraid of us."

"Are you ever going back to civilization?"

"Some day."

"Then this—this stunt of yours is not permanent?"

"We come as we need freedom."

"Do you know your countryman Bennet-Stokes?"

"Yes." The blunt affirmation lacked enthusiasm.

"There seems to be quite a difference between your sojourn in Tahiti and his," said Donald sarcastically.

"Most visitors to Tahiti come in wantonness—and fall to grief."

At that, Donald turned suddenly away, a stricture in his throat. It was a long moment before he was able to look again at Caldwell, who seemed to have noticed nothing, and resume the conversation. "You've lived here nine years?"

"Yes, about that."

"A long time! And you've never done anything else in all that time but your few tasks?"

"I walk a good deal. There is no wilder or freer place in all the world than the canyons back in the mountains from here. Once a month I go to Tautira or Vairao. But never to Papeete."

"You know the natives, then?"

"As well as any white man could know them."

"Is it true that they were cannibals?"

"Most observers have said no. But I think the whole Polynesian race once ate long pig, as they call the white man. The climate and food supply of any particular island or group decided just how much cannibalism was practiced. The Marquesas were bad. The Melanasian group worse. I've lived in both. In the New Hebrides and New Guinea there is cannibalism right to this day."

"What do you think the contact with whites has done to the Tahitians?"

"Debased, depraved, destroyed, a once happy people—the explorer first, then the sailor, the traders, then whalers and the missionaries, and the tourists. The Tahitians are a primitive race in captivity—they've been robbed. They've been given the white man's diseases, habits, foods, drinks, clothes. The white man's God has been imposed on them, but I never met a native who believed in his heart. Once hate was foreign to their nature. They lived from hand to mouth, a singing, jolly, happy people. Today there is little of the pure blood strain left. They have deteriorated in stature and strength, and they are confused—a bewildered people. The Chinese bread is a curse. The canned merchandise is a curse.

"The native will lie to you, so as to tell you what you want to know. He will steal anything he can lay his hands on. I don't blame him for that, for the fruits of these islands belong to him. But a subtle cunning underlies all his reactions to the white men who prey. Tahitians have a strange mental life beyond our ken, unless some peculiar circumstance makes it clear. Yet—and here's the paradox—some even went to the World War and died for France. Many of them! The Tahitian will care for, even love a white man's bastard. On the other hand, he abets, sometimes for drink or gain, the Chinese trader's seduction of little girls. You see little girls, no more than twelve years old, mothers, staggering around under the burden of slant-eyed infants. That always raises my gorge."

"It raises mine— You disapprove of missionaries?"

"No. Many of them have done much good. But not enough to offset the bad done by some of them, either. What I despise in some missionaries is their selfish, greedy graft. This spring I paid a visit to Bora Bora, over in the Leewards. I happened to arrive on a himone day. All the natives wore their Sunday best, except those who had none. The big himone house was over-flowing, with crowds standing outside. Two missionaries had come to collect dues. They harangued and persuaded. Then they called each native—by name—to advance to the table with his or her contribution to this worthy cause. One poor, ragged old beggar came up hesitantly to lay all he had, two francs, upon the table. He was scorned and flouted before them all. The next one, a prosperous-looking fellow, laid down a goodly amount. And he was hailed vociferously, lauded to the skies."

"Disgusting," said Donald shortly.

"Yes. But not so bad as this. Not long ago I visited Ikahupu. It's a long way by water, but if you are a mountaineer you can take this canyon here and climb through a wonderful region white men never see—not many miles across. Well, this day I slipped into a himone where funeral services were being held by a missionary. There I learned that when a man died, if his widow or kin contributed generously, his soul would be taken to heaven. His chance of getting there was proportionate to the offering. If his wife or children were too poor to pay—then the man's soul was damned. He must go to hell."

"It's a despicable way to teach religion, I agree. But what do you think will become of them, the Tahitians?" Donald asked.

"They will be absorbed by the Chinese. At first that observation disgusted me, as I can see it does you, Smith. I resented it. Romance and idealism were affronted. But I think now that the influx of Chinese blood will save the Tahitians from extinction. The Marquesans and others are dying out rapidly. But a new race will rise here—unless the French deport all Chinese, which might happen. In that case the brown people of Tahiti will perish."

"It strikes me that a nature man must have a unique opportunity to understand the Polynesians," returned Donald.

"Yes. They like me, though they think me balmy, because I'm not greedy like other white men. I have no ax to grind. I visit with them; often do some little service. I like to talk, and they like to talk. They have no work to do—neither have I. Time means nothing. They love to laugh—so do I. Then, most significant of all, I never look at their women, to lust after them. Native men hate white men who trifle with their women, just as they like and respect the one here and there who marries a girl."

"You've never had a native girl?" queried Donald.

"No, never," returned Caldwell. "God certainly never intended any man to live alone—even a nature man like myself feels the lack. It's the only drawback to an otherwise perfect life. But I never yielded to the urge, except just once, years ago. I asked a half-caste girl to live with me."

"She wouldn't?" asked Donald.

"She called me a big hunk of cheese," replied Caldwell, with his rolling laugh.

"Well! What was she like, this half-caste?"

"Haven't you seen Faaone?"

"*Faaone!* Oh, I—yes, surely. I've seen her."

"She was sixteen. For a white man to see Faaone then and not want her was to deny what I just admitted God intended man for. If he claimed he didn't, he would be a liar."

"What—what was she like?" queried Donald, with a constriction in his throat.

"She had in superlative degree all the physical charms with which nature has endowed the female of the species. But she was also evil. She hated white men, especially Englishmen—her father, by the way, is Bennet-Stokes. And she never lived with any white man long. Just long enough to destroy him! She was Tahiti incarnate. Or perhaps she had some terrible sexual power—too much for a white man."

"Yet you would have risked it?"

"Brother, there was nothing of reason or thought in my subjugation. I've often wondered at the strangeness of it. I suppose it was another manifestation of what chains me here—where the days and nights are too short—where I am happy without thinking—where I have no troubles, no regrets, no hopes, no past, no future, nothing but sweet life and the sun and stars!"

Donald asked no more questions. Finally he said: "Caldwell, I'm much obliged to you. My first impression of you was hardly more flattering than Faaone's. But you've got something that I wish I had. I wish to God I could live here, as you and your comrades do."

"Stay on, then, my brother," replied the nature man. "You will soon find the old scales, the old fetters, the old habits, falling off."

8

By living with the nature men and eating their food and listening to their endless talks, Donald tried to become one of them —their existence might be the best left for him. To that end, he gathered fruit with them and waded on the reef and along the shore, fishing with both line and spear. He hunted seashells and gathered flowers. When he became tired—which state day by day seemed to become more perceptible—he would retire to the camp and eat and lie around, basking naked in the sunshine. Sometimes he wondered why the police did not come to find him, but soon even that did not matter any more. If the nature men knew what had happened, they never revealed it to him.

However, it grew to be that his restful hours during the day and wakeful ones at night saw an increasing activity of consciousness, of thought and emotion. He began to fear these thoughts—vivid memories of his catastrophe. Only when he went out into the sun to be active, especially to fish, was he able to forget. He began to persist in these pursuits even after he and the nature men had secured enough for their simple wants, prolonging them until he was exhausted. The sun, the vivid marine creatures in the green water, the scent from the sea, the

eternal thunder of the outer reef and the music of the inner—
these blended somehow into the instinctive pursuit and capture
of his prey—kept the horror of his position at bay. But only the
primitive instincts, only physical exertions, had this power.
When forced to idleness, he was absolutely unable to induce
their spell.

Eventually, too, cooked fish and raw fish, octopus eaten raw
with lime juice, raw fruits, and concoctions that Donald stewed
himself—all began to pall upon him. The pangs of hunger became acute.

One day the giant Caldwell returned from Tautira with a
piece of meat and a loaf of bread wrapped in a newspaper. He
explained to his surprised comrades.

"Brother Smith is starving. My friend Charley had just butch-
ered. You should have seen his look when I asked for a piece of
beef. And the Chinese trader's when I bought the bread. Smith,
our reputation for complete abstinence is jeopardized."

"Thank you," said Donald warmly. "I do feel like a wolf. This
native diet just isn't for me."

"Well, eat this. You'll probably get a bellyache. Then, maybe,
you'll see how bad bread and meat are for you," responded
Caldwell, with his booming laugh.

While Donald broiled his meat over the red coals of coconut
hulls, Caldwell read the newspaper aloud. It was a *San Francisco Chronicle* of recent date. The giant read well, in a loud
voice. His two comrades listened intently. Donald did not want
to hear, but could not help it. The newspaper carried endless
news of the rackets, of gangster fights and holdups, of the kid-
nappings of children and the murders of men and rapes of
women, of the weekly massacre of pedestrians and motorists, of
the strikes of labor unions and the riots of the unemployed, of
corrupt politicians and their propaganda, of controversy over
the New Deal. Then the reader shifted to foreign news, reading
with evident satisfaction how England, due to the sacrifice of
her loyal subjects and governmental economy, was pulling out

of the Depression. He read of the dark and tragic place Germany had become, of a great people gone mad, of France and Italy at daggers drawn, of the menace of war from the Balkans.

Finally Caldwell dropped the paper as if it carried pestilence. "Smith, you ought to be glad you're here," he boomed. "Away from that God-awful mess!"

"Are you?"

"Yes. And I don't believe I'll ever go back. Europe is bad enough, but America is worse!"

"If I were a man, I'd be back there now," retorted Donald, stung.

"Why in God's name?"

"To fight the evils you just read about. Some men must rise to do it. Some *will!* I resent your poise, Caldwell, your air of calm superiority, your aloofness from all this hell you scorn. You're proud of your England. So is Bennet-Stokes. But what is *he* doing to help his country—what are *you* doing?"

"Brother American, I am proving something to myself," replied the Englishman, unruffled by Donald's passion.

Donald turned away, leaving the three nature men to fall into a tremendous argument, and carried his meat and bread and coconut milk to a spot on the shore out of hearing of the exasperating trio. "I don't fit in here," he soliloquized gloomily. "Hopeless for me to be a nature man. I'd be a nature fakir. . . . These men are kind. They took me in, but I can't stand them. If they're not crazy, I am. If they are really free—*happy*—then what in God's name am I?"

Night found him alone on the beach under the white stars, pacing the lovely shell-strewn strand, with the soft sea breeze playing upon him and the slow thunderous melody of the reef filling his ears. Eternal beauty all around, but all he felt was death in his soul. His mind wandered. He was back home, in the New England cottage that opened upon the green meadows and wooded hills, in his old room, with its white bed, its easy chair and inviting desk, his books and pictures. He heard the

90

piano downstairs and his little sister's voice. Gwen! And his mother . . . The scene shifted. Now he was downtown in New York after a long absence, meeting friends and acquaintances. Faces—glad faces, smiling eyes, warm handclasps, greeted him everywhere. How good to be among his own kind once more! To see respect and welcome! To move about old familiar places, the club, the hotel, the post office, where he went so often, hoping ever to receive a favorable letter from a publisher. Always in vain! But some day—some day, his dream told him.

The gay throngs, the brilliant lights of New York—the theaters with their audiences of beautiful women, bare-armed, diamond-bedecked, low-voiced, and charming—the nightclubs, bizarre, seductive, with their drinking crowds and bold dancers and heady music. He was in jostling crowds, under the rumbling elevated, walking bewildered in Macy's vast store. Dusk fell, and the streets grew wet and shiny with lights, and snow began to float down out of the opaque shadows above. It was New Year's Eve. A gaudy, rollicking, mischievous crowd streamed up and down Broadway, whistling, hooting, blowing horns. Showers of confetti mingled with the snowflakes. Donald felt the surge and sway of the roisterers and went their way, one of them.

Then, Winifred, radiant, exquisitely gowned, her violet eyes flashing with excitement and conquest, appeared in the picture. With her there, the rest faded into the background—*Winifred!*

And Donald came back to realities. The vision vanished. He stood alone upon the naked strand, under the pitiless stars, under the whispering palms, with the mockery of the lonely sea in his ears. This spot where he stood was the extreme end of Tahiti, the last sand-strip of that treacherous island—yet he could not abide here. He had no vestige of the peace of the nature men. He had not even the squalid occupation of the beachcomber. He was an outcast and a murderer, driven by the Furies, fleeing down the dim hall of desert night, his arms upflung to ward off the hags of remorse and regret. He had been dishonored. There was blood on his hands, and even murder had not eased the hurt in his heart. He was ruined, lost, his love debauched, his hopes devastated. There was nothing, nothing, nothing, to turn to, here or anywhere. He leaned against a palm tree to gaze out across the starlit sea. And he wept, strangled cries torn out of him by despair.

The relentless slow sea told him that it was so. The reef thundered it into his ears. The tinkle on the shore and the whisper in the leaves, soft sweet sounds—sounds the opposite of violence—reiterated it with damning quiet: He was nothing to that remorseless nature that the deluded Caldwell and his comrades imagined they worshipped.

No! cried some spirit from his depths. If that were so, why did he cling to life? How easy to end this misery! Once he had almost done it, and he never would have known a dying pang. But something had saved him. Suddenly before him he saw the image of Faaone—the native and white houri who had waited for him. And as suddenly, it seemed, he knew what he would do. He would go to Faaone. This calamity would wear itself out. He would go back and face whatever dark fate lay in store for him.

Donald clung to Faaone's image as he returned to the sleeping hut. He defied the mocking sea and the moaning wind and the whispering palms with it, and the looming shadows of the night—the specters, the traitors of his childhood. He kept it in his slumbers. And if, when at gray dawn he awakened, the shining illusion was gone, the intention was not.

He saw the nature men wrapped in slumber, prone on their mats, their dark peaceful faces turned to the morning light. "Useless! Wasters—from any point of view the world could take," he said to himself. "But not destroyers, such as I."

Putting the remaining meat and bread in the newspaper, he left the compound and with quick strides entered the canyon. At that early hour, it was almost dark in the tunnel made by the foliage from each side of the path that spread wide to join above. The stream, swollen by recent rains was a rushing torrent, unfordable in its lower reach. But it stepped down in a series of low rapids, and along its bank Donald made rapid progress, walking and leaping from stone to stone. At times he had to wade a few feet, the water swift and cold.

He had once ascended this stream, though not so far as the opening into the upper valley, the walls of which could be seen from below. More than once he had questioned Caldwell about where it led. His intention now was to follow its course up to the divide and then down another stream that was one of the headwaters of the great Tautira River. That the journey might be too much for him, he knew well. The fact did not deter him, though he had turned away from suicide. But he had to leave the nature men, and this was the other and unknown way out. He chose it.

For the most part the ascent of the canyon stream-bed was easy, though at times huge boulders obstructed his passage. The coconut palms soon failed, and he entered a jungle of huge maple trees with their fluted trunks, and wild hibiscus and breadfruit trees, laced together with giant lianas and broad-leaved vines and lacy creepers, forming an impenetrable wall.

There was something in this journey that acted upon Donald as had his intensive fishing and shell-hunting on the beach below. If he had a remnant of his old instinct for adventure left, it must have been aroused, for he went on swiftly, boldly, keen of eye, sure of foot.

The dark tunnel soon opened out into a wide lane full of subdued soft lights, silvery and misty above the borders of the widening stream. Through the mist, dim walls showed, rising sheer beyond the limit of his vision. A roar of waterfalls drowned the rush and babble of the river. Progress became easier along this less-precipitous course. The clear pools were full of shining nato, a beautiful fish that came in from the sea, and long brown eels and giant shrimps, although there were no birds, no animals along the singing stream. Blossoms of wild hibiscus, pale amber and yellow, floated like cups on the current. White moss, in thick bundles of threads, woven close and waving in the water, reached out from the banks.

When the sunlight, coming through some portal, dispelled the mist and opaque gloom, Donald found himself lost in a scene of savage grandeur. He had entered an amphitheater, a region too supernal for his credulity. He paused to look about him. Then, seized with a consciousness of the littleness of man and the sublimity of nature, he glued his eyes to the rocky way and went on. Not for a long while did he realize that the stream wound in wide circles down through this grand vale of solitude. He waded and walked, labored over and around stones and logs, hurrying to get out of the mountain-bowl, yet did not appear to make progress across it. Still he mounted higher all the time. And when at length a blaze of sunshine, hot and intense, struck him in the face, he looked up to see a narrow, sheer-walled cleft opening from the east, through which the sun burst into the valley, a long shaft of gold that widened from the aperture.

But hours and miles passed before he reached that portal. Meanwhile, the sun went up behind the pearl clouds that rolled in from the sea to hide the spear-pointed peaks and bridge the blue roof of the amphitheater with a lofty canopy. Thunder rolled from beyond the walls and dense black clouds, trailing veils of gray, showed through the gateway.

At last Donald came out upon a promontory, a step below the ragged V-shaped cleft, from which a white waterfall, ribbed and lacy, fell into a purple chasm. A drowsy hum floated up out of the depths. Through the portal, wide at close range, towering crags and monuments, green and gold to their sharp summits, directed Donald's gaze down and down to a gap of distant blue sea. He had reached the divide.

Sinking under a shelf of rock, he turned apprehensively to face the amphitheater. He had dared too much. Like dead scales his callousness sloughed off. Here, where perhaps only one other white man had been, and where few others besides himself in all the future ages would be, Donald gazed until he thought his heart would crack, and he would die from the overwhelming wonder of the scene.

Even as he watched, the panorama changed. Dark clouds swept over the rim, disintegrating and pushing the pearl canopy from its floating anchorage. And the gray veils of rain drooped over the green walls like curtains of silver lace, to hide the gateway and the waterfall and the towering slopes. Then they swept across the amphitheater to coalesce into one steel gray pall that swallowed up the ribbon stream, the stately rock-castle with green pennants flying, the mossy cliffs, and at last the floor and walls of the amphitheater itself.

Donald crept back into the shelter. Lightning flashes sent gleams of dim fire across the obscure space, and thunder crashed from the battlements. The hollow echoes filled the valley with a detonating din. When the last echo of one fearful crash had pealed back from below, another would split cloud and earth with steely flashes from on high, and again the terrifying echoes would bellow from wall to wall. The rain fell in a blinding torrent.

It was a storm that fit the savage heights of Tahiti. Such a storm was born there and did not pass out to sea. The gods and the devils of the elements appeared to be at war. Once the earth shook under Donald, and a deafening roar dwarfed all other sounds—a slipping avalanche, like the end of the world, it rolled away to leave the fury of the storm weak by comparison.

The storm ceased, not by passing away out over the sea, but by exhausting and spending itself against the peaks. Thin sheets of gray rain appeared to dry up as the clouds mushroomed and split to show bits of azure blue sky and lagoon that matched it except for the crawling curve of white. Once more the sun burst into the valley with rays and shafts of gold and amber.

From the towering peaks and domes, again tipped with

clouds of pearl, on all sides and from every wall poured down ropes of rain water, and sheets and cascades, and from the great green bulk of mountain that had born the brunt of the storm leaped a grand waterfall, curving far out from the cliff, falling sheer and clear, to drop white-curded a thousand feet, and spread thin and slow until it became downward smoke, never to reach the floor of the valley far below. And the valley was full of the sound of falling waters and slowly gathered rainbows.

Faint at first, they gathered color and intensity, to shine clearly, transparent—letting the green slopes and the gold shafts show through. The most sublime, a grand arch, curved from wall to wall, perfect in shape, glorious in hue, omniscient in promise. Donald reached out a trembling hand to see it rainbow-hued and unreal, as if detached from his arm. Another broad and vivid bow sprang from nowhere into the air, to vanish in the purple pit of the permanent waterfall. When one began to fade, another came to life. Across the valley, a black canyon mouth was filled with an arc that did not hide a plunging cataract.

Yet even as Donald gazed, the wondrous transfiguration began to pale. The waterfalls diminished, and the veils of misty rain yielded to the blazing sun—until, as if by magic, the valley was clear and hot once more, with thin steam beginning to rise from the rocks and trees.

The day was half-done, with the sun at its zenith and intense as molten steel. Donald ate the remainder of his meat and bread and drank from a pool in the rock. He must be on his way. But he seemed chained to that promontory. He had been divinely blessed, or cursed, by a glimpse of the savage nature that explained Tahiti physically, although it left the island's spirit, its meaning, darker than ever.

Once more the drowsy hum of murmuring waters made lingering and dreamy music. The vast amphitheater slept under the sun, a white and pitiless master, giver and taker of life.

Suddenly Donald divined that he would never leave Tahiti.

96

White men had come to this green mound in the blue Pacific and, leave or stay, they had never been the same again. Idleness, uselessness, forgetfulness, ruin, and death had come to most who remained. All but the last had already come to him. That he must hold at bay until he had solved the secret of Tahiti —only that one left of all his passionate desires!

A hot wind blew through the gateway, laden with the fragrance of flowers and the faint tang of the sea. He saw the broad leaves of the fei fei trees move in the breeze. A somber mournfulness permeated the solitude, upon which the sharp peaks, cleaving the blue, looked down implacably. Donald felt himself a prisoner of forces of fierce wild nature that hid under a mask of everlasting beauty and color and majesty. The world of civilization and achievement, all that he had been born to, was for naught. The truth, whatever that was, lay in the hot breath of the sun, in the strong and steady wind that fanned his heated face, in the encompassing mountains, which were in turn encompassed by the eternal sea.

At length he rose, crossed the jutting bench, and climbed, wearily now, up toward the pass. He did not look back at the vast hole out of which he had climbed. He had lost it, he knew, for always, but he feared that—if he looked—the scene below would hold him spellbound indefinitely, and the rugged canyon would surely be his grave.

Far down through the thick green, he emerged upon a brook that ran away from the divide. He followed it hour after exhausting hour, while it gathered volume and strength from intersecting streams. It entered finally a narrow canyon defile, the gleaming walls of which slanted far above him. He waded. And, when the walls closed in upon the deep and rushing water, he swam and floated on the current. Wide stretches afforded him a respite. He walked and recovered breath, but his strength was waning rapidly.

At last the bare split in the mountain opened out into a wider, less precipitous valley. Here golden oranges and limes, red bananas, green walls of bamboo, and shiny clumps of fei fei, with their bunches of ripening fruit, appeared, by some quirk of nature, to thrive in a fierce and tangled jungle. It was late in the afternoon when, bloody and wet, about ready to fall and gladly give up the struggle, he fell out of the tangle onto a well-defined trail. The tracks of barefoot natives showed in the mud.

With renewed strength he plodded on. This trail would lead somewhere, perhaps down to Tautira, surely to the huts of natives. The afternoon waned. And the sun, long behind the great looming slope to his left, came out over the edge of the mountain wall. From time to time Donald's dulled senses caught a distant sound that he at first took to be thunder. But its return at regular intervals, and its resounding roar, proved it to be surf beating on the reef. He was approaching the north coast of the peninsula.

He lost the trail in deep green weeds, so thick he could almost walk upon them. But they sank under his weight, and abandoning that course, he floundered off into the jungle toward the sound of running water. He was stopped by a wide, deep river, its shining surface dotted with floating hibiscus blossoms and great golden breadfruit leaves. Wearily he tried to retrace his steps. But it was no use. He stumbled on, through a dark mapee swamp, where the huge trees obscured the light and the mud reached his knees, into a banana forest. Again he espied footprints, but could not locate a trail.

Finally the sound of running water once more revived his failing hope and he pushed toward it. Through ferns higher than his head he glimpsed a glade beyond, bright with the gold of the setting sun. The murmuring water drew him onward, until, fainting almost, he made one last desperate lunge and came out upon the bank of a pool shimmering like molten gold.

He staggered, sank to his knees, then looked up, startled by a scream. A figure stood in the pool. It was a naked woman, her form a darker gold against the glowing pool. She held a towel with which she quickly covered herself. She was young, too light-skinned to be a full-blooded native. Long black tresses rippled down from her small head. Flashing eyes, large and black, fastened upon Donald.

"You!" she gasped, and a slow smile transformed her face. "How long it has taken you to come!"

"Faa—one!" In Donald's darkening sight she appeared as a nymph in a dream. Suddenly she swung the towel behind her and stood triumphant, with arms uplifted, her honey-hued breasts erect. A seductive loveliness stole over her face. Her slender, yet voluptuous, form was limned gold against the light as Donald slid off into blackness.

part II
FAAONE

9

Faaone gazed down upon her bed where Donald Perth lay, the wreck of the handsome young man who had brought out the strange passion in her. He had been days under her care, ever since, fevered and spent, he had collapsed on the bank of her bathing pool. She had had him carried into her house, and there had ministered to him. While he had been consumed with fever and delirium, she had felt him to be like a little boy, alone, lost, helpless. But now he was conscious, and his fine blue eyes held the light of reason.

"Faaone?" he whispered.

"Yes, Donald. Who else?" she replied, and sat down on the bed beside him.

He gazed at her, slowly accepting her as reality. Then he looked about the clean spacious room, at the bed, and the spotless red and blue checkered coverlet. He felt the soft sleeves of the pajamas he had on, and then his face, which was clean-shaven.

"What—happened, Faaone?"

"Nothing much. I knew you were coming. I had the men put up this new house last month, and I moved all my things from the beach below. My mother and our people and friends live just below on the river. They thought you were dead. But the tupapa'us told me you had not died. When I heard there was another white man living with the nature men, somehow I knew it was you."

"I was just about dead when you found me, if I remember. You saved my life."

"I do not know. You had the fever. My mother worked over you. And I nursed you."

"Have you been here with me? How long is it?"

"Days. I never left you. I have been sleeping there on a mat. I will sleep with you, now you are better."

"You've been very kind," he returned, taken aback by this forthright offer. "But I have to go back, when I am well, to face them."

She smoothed his brow and ran her fingers through his damp hair. "If you go back to Papeete, that life will destroy you," she said vehemently. "And if it does not, Papeete is still death! All the natives along there are friends or relatives of Tavarie. They cannot be trusted."

"But I must go back, I must—"

"There is no one to face, Donald, except ghosts," Faaone said. "You were cleared. Your blonde vahine took the stand and said Tavarie tried to rape her, and you saved her from him. She did that even when they had found your car at the end of the road in Teahupoo and thought you had killed yourself. I think she really loved you, though she went home on the next boat."

"I guess she did. But that's all over now." As if he had just realized the import of her words—and his—he fell silent and turned his face away from her. "I can't stay here in any case," he said at last, with weak stubbornness.

"But why not? Did she break your heart?"

He lay quiet for a little, as if soothed by her caressing hand. Then he said weakly, "I still murdered a man—for no real reason."

104

"But a lot of people, at least my people, do not feel that way," she argued. "Tavarie had been in trouble before. It must have happened to him sooner or later, as it did to his father. It is over. You are free now—and I can be the Reef Girl for you," she went on softly, leaning over him. "I have never been that for any man."

"What have you been?" he demanded.

"Just a native girl."

"But, Faaone, I have heard about you, how you destroyed the others."

"Yes, I hated them. Because of my mother! Because they came to Tahiti to revel, to lounge and feast and guzzle. To use Tahiti to satisfy their lusts! To buy the native girls and then desert them."

"I know. You had cause. But Faaone, I'm not that kind of man. And I'm only a shell—as you see. You couldn't avenge Tahiti any more through me. You don't love me."

"No. I could not love any white man—or native. But I shall make *you* love *me*. I can be all of Tahiti to you."

"I don't doubt that. It's why I must go, Faaone."

He tried to raise himself, only to fall back.

"You are too weak, Donald. For now, at least, you must stay." Again she caressed his brow, and, as he looked up at her, leaned down and touched her lips to his. "You must stay," she repeated softly. "You must stay."

When Donald was asleep, Faaone went into the kitchen. It was a spacious, light room, new and clean like the rest of the house. The thresholds were built high to keep out the pigs and chickens. Tamu, a neighbor, was working on a stone and clay stand, waist-high, upon which she could cook with charcoal or coconut husks. There was, in addition, a kerosene stove, at which Faaone was not adept. In fact she was not adept as a housekeeper, having relied upon her mother almost entirely. It was needful now that she learn. This new white man whom she had taken in would make a vast difference. He would not have

105

the money that made her mother and all her kin worship white men, and there were neighbors down the river, friends and relatives of Tavarie, who hated him. She thought she hated him, too, yet she wanted him, and ever since the ball at the French Colonial she had known that he would come to her. At last he had come, not the lithe athletic young man with the wistful eyes and sweet smile, but broken, older, and dazed somehow, for the present an object of pity.

"Tamu, have you finished that?"

"Tomorrow, Faaone."

"Always tomorrow. You finish it today."

She went out to call Tupa, her six-year-old nephew. The sun shone dazzlingly white and hot; the waterfall hummed, and the banana leaves rustled in the sultry breeze; the crystal stream glided by the grassy bench down toward the calling river. Frangipani bushes, white and gold, banked luxuriantly at the back of the level bench, and a low spreading flambuoyant tree flamed red over the thatched roof of her house.

Faaone had chosen this site for its solitude. Hers was the last habitation up the river. The fei trail that passed her door went on into the jungle. Down below were the homes of her mother and relatives, the little taro gardens and banana groves of the neighbors, and finally the road, where the native colony Fitieu straggled along the beach.

As Faaone waited for Tupa, she looked across the valley at the white waterfall, which broke three times in its descent from the high notch, and up the river at the purple peaks. Since childhood she had known this scene of jungle and mountain and dancing water. Today the green walls loomed with lofty aloofness, less protectively than usual it seemed, as if withholding a judgment. In broad daylight, under the blazing sun, there was not the brooding mystery and menace that came with night. But there were silent voices. And she heard with her native ears what her white blood repudiated.

Tupa came running out of the ferns. He was the son of her

unmarried sister, a slight urchin, who, with his big head and deformed little body, looked much older than six years. He was naked except for a ragged shirt. He had great jewel eyes, dark and bright.

"Come in, Tupa," she said, taking his hand. "I want you to watch my white man while I go down to the store. Be very quiet, and fan the flies away while he sleeps. I will fetch you candy."

Tupa beamed as he took the red fan she gave him and squatted beside the bed where Donald lay asleep. Faaone put a finger to her lips, then opened a chest to get what money she had. It was little enough. Money meant nothing to her. It was something she could not keep. But she had many pieces of gold and many pearls, and some jewels which she could sell in Papeete or use to pay the Chinese storekeeper in Fitieu.

Faaone glanced at Donald and then walked closer to peer down. With his eyes closed, the physical frailty and the spiritual havoc were accentuated. Tahiti had delivered him into her hands almost too late. As she turned to leave, she brooded on that golden-haired, blue-eyed, white-skinned girl who had destroyed him, but then had saved him from a French prison or perhaps even worse. Since Donald's coming, Faaone had often remembered her.

It required effort for Faaone to go, but there were supplies to purchase and plans to make while on her way to the store. With her swift, free stride, she left the clearing and took the trail toward the village. The hum of bees and the chatter of mynah birds filled the sultry gold-flecked air. In low places the trail was lined by ferns and wet moss.

Faaone had never gone barefoot like her people. Even wading on the reef and swimming in the lagoon or surf, she always wore something to protect her small feet. Her inordinate vanity had been born in her, but education among the whites had taught her how to preserve and enhance her beauty. She had learned, too, of creams and oils and cosmetics, but these luxuries she used sparingly and dubiously. The sun and the river and the reef, with the simple Tahitian diet, constituted Faaone's recipes for beauty.

The trail came out upon the river, which here sparkled and babbled over wide pebbly bars, past stony pools, and wound out of sight into the jungle. Tall orange trees with huge, round, green oranges thickly clustering and silver bronze breadfruit trees and coconut palms marked the approach to the clearing where her mother and numerous kin lived on both sides of the river. Broad-leaved taro plants extended along a low flat just above high-water mark. Near the trail, a melon patch spread under the palms. The thatch-roofed huts stood on higher ground, and a grassy open space, shaded by palms, sloped gently from them to the river.

Faaone came out of the silence of the jungle into the action and color of native life. Dogs barked at her approach, attracting the attention of the naked, playing children. There were sleepy cats in the sun and haltered pigs grunting in the shade. Horses stood knee-deep in the ferns. Women were washing their linens and pounding poi at the mouth of a running brook. On the grass in the sun gleamed white sheets and red pareus and blue dresses.

Of the children who ran like quail to meet her, screaming their delight, the foremost was Frangi, Faaone's favorite among her numerous relatives. Frangi was twelve, still a slip of a girl. Her eyes were large and black, and her hair rippled down her slender shoulders in a lustrous brown mass.

"Frangi," said Faaone, "go up to my house and stay with Tupa till I come back. Be very quiet. I will fetch you some candy."

"Yes, Faaone," cried the child eagerly, and was off like a flash.

Faaone went on, with the children dropping back, one by one, to their play. Her mother's house stood at the end of the long clearing, the first one in from the road. It was a frame structure standing high on posts and was painted blue. The tin roof was red. All around it were hibiscus bushes, frangipani

108

trees, and tiare-tahiti. The paths of coral sand were lined by trimmed hedges of russet, heliotrope, and rose leaves. A huge clump of yellow-stemmed bamboos drooped over the wide porch with its French trellis-work.

As Faaone approached this pretentious and gaudy house—the gift of Bennet-Stokes—the big gray land crabs all along the trail watched her with sharp eyes, plopping back into their holes at her near step. Matureo, her mother, sat on the porch, stitching colored figures on a white cloth. A thin curtain blew out of the open door. She was still a handsome woman, but there were traces of havoc on her strong dark face. Apparently she was alone.

"Matureo, I am going to Hing's to buy food."

Her mother laid aside her work and fastened large somber eyes of faded brilliance upon Faaone.

"Daughter, you mean to keep this white man with you? To live with him—cook for him?"

"Donald is sick, friendless."

"He will grow well soon. He is young. If you feed him white man's food and keep drink from him, he will be able to leave soon. You will send him away?"

"I shall keep him."

"He has nothing. He will never work. He could not ply the nets or spears. All Tavarie's people hate him, and so will yours when they are poor again. This will be bad for you, my daughter."

"It may be good. I cannot tell."

"Then—at last—you love a white man?" her mother asked with scorn.

"No, Matureo, I do not love him."

"Why, then, take in this enemy of your people?"

"Because it was to be."

"Only evil can come of it. To you—to me—to us all. Already it is known. Benstokes will learn. He will withhold the gifts that you could gain for yourself—for me."

"I would starve before I would take a franc from him. If you dare, I shall turn from you."

"But, daughter, we will be poor again."

"You can live as once you lived—like our people. And I can too, while Donald grows strong again."

"Yes, *I* can, but you—never. You are white in all but one way, Faaone. And the years of your generosity have spoiled me and your sisters, brothers, our kin, even the children. They cry for Chinese bread and tinned beef."

"But I *can*, mother."

"Then you are changed, daughter. But I do not believe it. Benstokes was here again today. He is kind, patient. He loves you. He will make us rich if . . ."

"Would you let me go to him?" demanded Faaone, passionately.

Matureo spread wide her strong hands and shrugged her plump shoulders. "My daughter, you will not marry a brown man. Your white lovers you have destroyed, so that no more will come to you. Benstokes could save us—and it would not be needful that he live forever."

The unspoken threat was not lost upon Faaone. But it did not mitigate either her hate or her scorn. Her mother could drown a lifetime of both in the thought of money; she could not.

"Faaone, sorrow will come of this pale white man. Heed me before it is too late."

"Sorrow. Have I ever known otherwise? It is not happiness I seek. Matureo, you brought me into the world, my soul native and my heart white. I am two persons. If Donald could make me one I—I would . . ."

"He cannot make you anything but misery. Poverty is that to natives who have been led away from their simple lives."

"Mother, I am rich, if I sell my gold—my pearls."

"Yes, but you never will. If you do that for him—Aue!—you love him indeed."

"I tell you no," cried Faaone, moved to anger.

"You lie, even to she who gave you life."

"If I do, Matureo, it is the Tahitian woman in me who is false."

"Listen, or you will be all false. Care for this sickly white if you will, but only until he is well. Then send him away. I will endure the wrath and stay the tongues of our people. But Benstokes I cannot fool for long. He will set the devil upon you."

"Enough, Matureo," returned Faaone, violently. "I owe none of you duty or loyalty. To appease your hate I gave in to hate, and worse. I let loose in me that devil you speak of. I am neither a white woman nor a brown one. My hunger for a child—for my own flesh and blood—can never be satisfied, because love was destroyed in me. Beware of Benstokes's words and money! If he turns you and all of my people against me, it will be an evil day for him."

Faaone swept down the trail, deaf to her mother's cries and those of the children trooping under the palms. It was worse than she had anticipated. Those days she had been so occupied with nursing Donald had already seen gossip up and down the road. Bennet-Stokes had been there, insidious with his power, money, and wine. Already Matureo had stifled her hate enough to be willing to offer her daughter to him. He would work on the deep resentment and passion for revenge of the relations and friends of Tavarie and buy her own people with money. Oh, Faaone saw the plot clearly! But, instead of weakening her purpose, the opposition inflamed her. She did not love Donald, but she would not let him go!

Among her people Faaone had been regarded as a princess and benefactor and worshipped as such. This morning, as she passed down the road through the village, no smiles greeted her, except from the children. Some of the men, idling on the porches or under the trees, watched her with somber speculative eyes. The glad and gracious hail from her own sex was wanting. She read a question in the dark eyes of the young women—what was she going to do? But in the stony eyes of the older women there was no question. Faaone had taken up with

111

the white slayer of Tavarie. This district was the one in which the son of the Sweet-Smelling Man had been born. He had been a chief among these men and god to the women. Faaone felt an alien wall confronting her, and the fact that she was a half-caste had nothing to do with it. To propitiate them and win them back, she would have to put Donald out and scatter manna again among them who already owed her much.

Hing, the sharp-eyed little Chinese storekeeper, who had always been her good friend, received Faaone with bows and words of welcome. Hing operated truck gardens along the road and a meat market in Papeete; he could order anything that he did not have in his store and it would arrive from town on the evening bus. Faaone left his store laden with about all she could carry. Retracing her steps she did not look to the right or left, but, at the end of the village where the lagoon cut in close to the road and a stone bridge crossed the brook, she laid down her load to rest a moment. She had first seen the light near this spot. Though she had been taken away from it in early childhood, she had always remembered the clear brook tumbling over the gray stones, the long half-moon beach of black sand, the yellow coral, and the sounding roar of the reef, which in later years had given her the name of Reef Girl. These things, and the gliding river, the changing waterfalls, the purple canyons, and unscalable savage peaks had deeper roots in her blood even than the people of whom she was only half a part.

On the way back up the trail the children waylaid her once more, and her mother came out and found a moment to importune. There would be no end to this, Faaone thought. Tiare, another of her relatives, relieved her of some of her burdens and helped her home with them. She was fifteen, dusky and plump, a giggling girl who showed as always only a merry friendliness toward Faaone. She would be helpful in the uncertain days to come.

Tupa and Frangi ran out to meet them and received their candy with ecstatic joy.

"Faa, he woke up," said Tupa, earnestly, as if to defend his guardianship. And Frangi shyly said she was not afraid of Faaone's new white man.

Faaone found Donald sitting up in bed.

"Donald! You are better?"

"Yes. I think, if I had a drink, I could get up," he replied, smiling at her.

"Water?" she queried, smiling back at him.

"Hardly. I want a drink, not a bath."

"I fetched you some port wine."

"All right. Anything to take this taste out of my mouth."

Faaone went into the kitchen to unpack her basket. Tiare was unwrapping heavy parcels. Tamu had finished the fire stand and had left a smouldering bed of red charcoals upon it. The smoke smelled good to Faaone. She opened one of the bottles of port and, filling two glasses, went in to Donald.

"Here, Donald, to your good health—and our happiness," she said.

He looked up at her with a skeptical, sad smile. Then he drank.

"Faaone, who are the nice kids you left with me?"

"Tupa is my nephew. Frangi is some sort of cousin, I guess. They are my favorites of a flock of youngsters."

"It took a long time for me to get them to talk. But I did finally. Then I could understand only a little. Frangi is pretty. Isn't she part white?"

"They say not, but I suspect she is."

"While you were gone a man came to the door. He was peering in, but left when he saw the kids. A tall, dark fellow, not young. There were leaves and bits of fern stuck to him, and I saw through the door that he had set down a load of fei. Faaone, I mention it because I didn't like the look in his eyes. I spoke, but he only grunted and backed out."

"Tall and dark? Not young?" repeated Faaone. It sounded like Moto, a cousin of Tavarie's. Faaone did not like the inci-

113

dent, but she said only, "So many natives are tall and dark."

"Faaone, I got the idea from the children that my being here is resented by your people," he said gravely.

"Yes, it is. But that makes me only more determined to keep you."

"But you've done enough for me. I shouldn't stay."

"Donald, tell me honestly. Are you an outcast from your people?"

"I suppose I am."

"Well, I shall be too, presently. I am bitterly angry with my mother. With most of them. I gave them too much. Now that I shall have no more to give, they will turn against me. We outcasts belong together."

"It's not a fair bargain."

"Yes it is, if I want it."

"Faaone, I'm not quite a beggar. I have a little income."

"You would *keep* me?"

"If I stayed I'd prefer to pay my board, at least. And if you have no money . . . But, Faaone, I tell you I should go, before I get well enough to—to want you."

"That you want me makes me happy."

"If I fell in love with you now it would be terrible."

"That's what I want. For you to love me terribly."

"But why? Why? I'm just a poor dreamer."

"I thought I knew why, but—I don't know, Donald. Maybe I have an instinct to love someone terribly. I have never loved anyone, except my mother, and that was long ago. And the children. But it has been impossible for me to love a native man. I have refused to marry Punerie, who is a good man from this village, because I cannot return his love for me. And the white men I have known— Oh, pigs! Pigs!"

"Faaone, what will become of you?"

"I am still the Reef Girl."

114

"Could you sink to the level of those Papeete harlots who hang around the dock on ship day?"

Faaone's lips framed a hot and scornful denial, but his earnest, wistful look gave her an inspiration. "My beauty will not last forever. My pride will die with it. I cannot always be the Reef Girl. Besides, as soon as I cease to provide for my selfish people, they will not want me."

"Faaone! If I thought I—"

"Don't think, Donald. See if you can walk a bit, while I make us something to eat."

From the kitchen door Faaone watched him leaning on a stick beside the pool. Tupa was with him, eagerly pointing out some fish or eels. Donald had put on the white shirt and trousers she had procured for him from Hing's. He looked very thin and frail, but his hair shone in the sun, and he had not lost his air of distinction. He would stay, to save her from a harlot's fate. He was gentle, good, loving. No doubt, always he had sacrificed himself. Yes, he would stay.

For this occasion, Faaone set her table out on the wide porch facing the waterfall and fetched her linen and pretty tableware and the few pieces of silver she owned. And, when the meal was ready, she called Donald. He needed to lean upon her to reach the porch. His face was pale and wet with sweat. Tupa supported him on the other side.

"Tupa showed me some dandy fish," Donald said. "Silver and dark, a little like our trout. Nato, he called them. He threw in bits of wood to make the nato rise. Faaone, I wonder, would they take a fly? I mean artificial flies tied on a hook to look like a natural fly—"

"But I understand, Donald. I tie my own. And I love to fish for nato."

"What?" he queried blankly.

"I love fishing almost as passionately as I love swimming. I use flies for nato and also for reef fish. I make my own tackle, including my flies."

"Well, of all things! *You*, Faaone!" he exclaimed, with great surprise and pleasure.

"Yes, *I*, Faaone!" she retorted. She had not before seen him glad.

"Will you take me fishing?"

"Surely, as soon as you are well."

She placed him at the table. "Tupa," she said, "you can eat with us. Sit there near the step and keep the dogs out." She called Tiare, who was to serve. "Donald, you must eat sparingly. I have beef soup for you and rice and milk, real milk. Have you eaten poi?"

"No. But I lived on fruit out with the nature men. I liked breadfruit, until I became sick of it. Faaone, this is a treat. I'm afraid it's not going to be easy for me to run off."

"I won't let you."

He ate so hungrily and with such relish that Faaone had difficulty restraining him. Afterward she arranged a mat and pillows in her big porch rocker, where he appeared content to lie back, exhausted.

"Do you like this place?" she asked.

"It's wild and lonely and beautiful. How near are your people?"

"Half a mile down through the jungle. I used to come here to bathe. I like this high bench above the valley. This little waterfall here and that big one up the middle canyon never fail. But after a storm you can see waterfalls everywhere."

"Faaone, I could gladly lie here forever," replied Donald dreamily, as he drifted off to sleep.

He did not mean it yet, but he would, she thought. She sent Tupa off with a knife to cut bamboo poles, slender, straight— light ones that she would trim while they were green and then leave to harden in the sun. If Donald liked to fish she would make it a passion. She decided the hour was one to emphasize with flowers and took a basket and went to gather them. Around her clearing, sweet-smelling blossoms were almost as abundant as leaves. She picked flambuoyant, frangipani, tiare-tahiti, and white jasmine blossoms. Returning to the house she piled them in a fragrant heap on the porch and sat down on a mat, cross-legged like the natives, to weave leis. Tiare came shyly to help. They whispered while Donald slept. Purple shadows began to form low down in the clefts and chasms, while the dark line on the opposite walls slowly rose to absorb the gold. When Donald awoke Faaone offered him his choice of the four leis.

"They are all beautiful," he said.

"Each has a different meaning."

Donald accepted the white jasmine, to her secret gratification. Of all the leis, he had chosen the one meaning hope. Then she gave him a sprig of white jasmine and knelt, bending her head to him.

"Donald, put it in my hair above my right ear. I have never worn one there."

"Don't I remember seeing a flower over your ear?" he asked.

"Yes, but it was my left."

"I have forgotten the language of Tahitian flowers." He fastened the white jasmine in her hair. "What lovely hair you have, Faaone! What does it mean—over the right ear?"

"Ask Tiare."

Donald turned inquiring eyes upon the shy maiden.

"Faaone is telling that she has found a lover."

Later, Faaone sat alone on the porch step, listening. The intense quiet of the canyon made acutely clear the dirge of the ebb tide, the low hum of insects, the soft flow of moving waters, the mysterious whisper of approaching night. Tupa and Frangi had left at the first fall of dusk, and Tiare had left before full darkness, for she dared not meet the tupapa'us on the jungle trail. Donald had gone to bed, fallen into his first deep slumber.

Faaone wished despairingly that she had been an all-white or all-brown woman. It was the conflict in her that betrayed first one side and then the other. To have been born like his sweetheart, Winifred, fair-skinned and golden-haired, one of those fortunate vahines of that wonderful America, rich and cultured, possessor of marvelous gowns and gems, but good instead of bad —how Faaone longed to have been so blessed! But despite her ten years and more of school in New Zealand, and the efforts of the Englishwomen of breeding and education who ran it— despite the change those years had made in her life—she was still a native, still slave to the prejudices of her people.

With all the white teaching, the white part of her had failed to be superior to or stronger than that other, darker self. In fact, as the years sped by, the reef and the sea, the jungle and the river, the flowers and the mountains, the legion of tupapa'us— all except the people with their scarred and ulcered ankles and their flat feet—drew her closer and closer, inevitably away from the education in her past. And if she could not think wholly with the native mind, intangible fears still absorbed her despite her efforts to dismiss them. She felt a grand scorn for her human enemies, but she dreaded the spirits of the darkness, the hidden dead things that came to life at night. Far up the valley, over the divide, was the vast bowl, walled in by mountains, where the first people had lived and fought the black men who came from far-off islands. Their spirits wandered abroad at night and some of them were tupapa'us.

A radiance as from a flame shone above the notch of the mountains opposite, where the waterfall gleamed softly, and the disc of the moon appeared. Rising, it gradually lost its tinge of red.

Faaone shivered, and slipped noiselessly into the house. Dimly she could make out Donald lying prone on the bed. She drew the coverlet up over him. And with a pause, to peer at her charge and to listen for she knew not what, she prepared to sleep. The hard mat on the cold floor was not to know her body this night, nor again. Very gently, so as not to awaken Donald, she slipped into the bed. She wanted the touch of his hand. But she settled herself softly, closed her eyes, and yielded to the native gift for sleep.

When she awakened, the moonlight streamed unearthly into the room. She felt very small in the big bed and dared not reach for her sisters, Turea and Arearea. There was something that prevented her! She wanted to cry out for her mother. The night was as silent as the cave of the skulls. Then a rustle outside prickled her skin with cold darts, and there was a sound like a barefoot step on the porch. It was heavy and jarred the floor. A darkness snuffed out the moonlight—but as she lay there, her tongue cleaving to the roof of her mouth, the silver light streamed in again.

The tupapa'us were outside. She saw a white shadow glide by the window—a form so transparent that she could see the silver foliage through it. A mournful wind sighed down the valley. It breathed through the house, stealthily stirring her hair. Tiny feet pattered across the floor. The place where the white shadow had been grew black again.

Faaone started upright in bed with the terror of childhood upon her. The room was as light as day. Donald lay beside her, his face like stone, peace or death upon it. Then she heard him breathe. The night wind was rasping in the crooks of the breadfruit trees. Rats ran over the porch, rustled in the thatched roof. The soft thud of a hoof sounded from the grass. There were no gliding shadows, no footsteps or tupapa'us. Nothing except the native in her, awakening from nightmare!

She lay back in relief. She was not alone. Donald's profile, pale and sharp as chiseled coral, stood out against the gloom. Faaone reached out, almost to touch his hair. But then the shadow crowded out the silver light once more. There was a drumming in her ears—a sound she had never heard before. They had returned. A rolling, noiseless, intangible mass came down upon her. It was like a cloud through which she could see. A ghost walked by the house. From the depths of the river bottom shrilled an eerie cry. It was inhuman, but she knew it for Tavarie's pealing cry to his fishermen at the nets. Tavarie was there in his tupapa'u.

Faaone started to rise, but sighting a thing in the doorway she sank back. It was a thin shape, black against the returning moonlight. Black tapa-cloth over a skeleton! No! She saw a skull like a burned coconut, with hollow eyes, black and as deep as the sea. How long and slim this shape! It glided in like a blown banana leaf. Long slim black arms reached out with clutching hands, ghastly gray in hue—the hands of a leper. The tupapa'u of the lepers!

With a scream Faaone wrenched herself up. The horror vanished. Donald rose on his elbow to peer fearfully at her.

"What? Faaone! Faaone!" he cried, reaching for her. "You screamed. What frightened you?"

"A dream—I guess," she faltered, and sank back to cling to him with trembling hands, and laid her head against him. "I forgot I was not alone. . . . Donald, hold me—love me—"

For a moment he hesitated. Then suddenly his arms embraced her. His voice, muffled at first, became stronger. "Faaone, I've been such a fool. I think I loved you from the first day, but I was afraid of myself—of you—of that side of me that came out the night—the night I killed Tavarie."

All at once her fears had vanished. "Donald, my lover," she whispered. "Look at me." She sat up and with a single gesture slipped off her pareu, revealing her magnificent body, cream-colored in the moonlight that streamed in from the window.

Then his arms were around her, his lips hot and searching at her mouth and her breasts. A fire seemed to run through him into her body. It was a passion she had never felt before, and it enveloped her. He was no longer the shy, awkward boy but her vibrant lover. Their bodies locked together, they sank down on the bed in an ecstasy of fulfillment, which neither of them had ever known before.

Later they lay quietly together, their naked bodies touching, relaxed and content. Faaone gently ran her fingers along his cheek and through his hair.

"For a while, I thought you would never love me—that you were a pédé."

"I was only a fool. Somehow I never knew love could be like this."

"I love you too. I never believed I could love a white man, but . . . You are my malahine."

The night closed around them like a soft blue veil, and all was peaceful.

Late the next afternoon, while Donald rested, Faaone went down to her family in the village. She was clad in her flaming red gown, and she wore the white flower over her right ear. She found her people among a gossiping crowd, waiting for the himone hour. Her mother wailed her grief; her sisters lashed at her with stinging tongues; her men kin spread their hands with expressive grins of resignation. She felt, rather than observed, the mute scorn of Tavarie's people. And Punerie, who had never given up his hope of marrying her, walked away from her into the forest, his stride, his posture indicative of final defeat.

Thus, defiantly, she dispelled their doubts. She tried to gauge her future by what she read in their faces. It seemed a matter of family—the weakness of her own and the hatred of Tavarie's. Faaone thought she would lose but little from the latter. But, though her imperious pride had brooked no interference with her peculiar ways of living, yet she knew that she was dependent upon her family and friends and upon this place of her birth for the things that made life significant. Had she broken with them forever?

121

Coming home she hurried, for after sunset the dusk fell almost at once to yield to night, and she had the same fears as those that made Frangi and Tiare fly like birds down the shadowed aisles. Only on the porch, with Donald asleep and dependent upon her protection, could she keep at bay spirits of the dark and the assailing fears that abide within.

10

❊

❊

❊

The eternal summer days of Tahiti passed with their rose-pink clouds at dawn, their white-hot sun and glooming gray palls of rain, their steaming jungle-hours and trade-wind-rippled lagoon and spindrift flying on the reef, and their golden sunsets flashing wondrous lights across the sea. There were moments when Faaone could have touched the first deep happiness of her life had she been free of dread and doubt. The dread was of invisible hands in the dark reaching to take Donald from her; the doubt was of herself, of a passion that no longer seemed related to hate. By day she had become a watching creature, suspicious of the wind in the palms, of the rustle of lizards in the thatch; by night a woman driven to use her beauty to enslave her white man.

In a few weeks Donald had gained back almost all the lithe strength she had admired. His skin had burned brown. He could work for hours in the garden before the hot sun made him desist. He never tired of trying to master the intricacies of nato fishing or wading on the inner reef with spear or pole. And as for his love of her—Faaone hugged to her soul the bitter truth that her beauty and abandon, the tricks of the South Sea woman, the exotic and savage passion born in her, had won his worship. Donald Perth was hers, body and soul. He would never leave her. He had no thought of a future without her and infinite scorn for the hidden peril that menaced him through her people. He was gentle and passionate with her by turns, proud of her beauty, believing in her love—wholly different, she felt certain, from other lustful men for whom she had degraded herself.

Yet awareness that he had no happiness outside the fleeting bliss in her arms grew and grew with Faaone's every thoughtful hour. She had not saved Donald Perth to make him happy, she argued to herself. She had done it to add fuel to the consuming fire in her blood! But, when she caught him sitting in the shade, his sad blue eyes fixed on the far rim of the sea or looking through the purple mountains at something beyond her knowledge, she was jealous of what was in his mind, of his past, of his people, of that golden-haired girl who had brought this havoc to his life. When he was in these moods, she could not reach him. She knew that only this Tahitian life of his was hers and that in his heart he lived in the past.

Someday, thought Faaone, when Benstokes had tired of his pursuit, or she had leashed the savage in her and the hate that had begotten hate had died, then she would discover for Donald the Tahiti of her ancestors, before the shadow of white men had fallen upon it.

One day, after they had been together some time, Donald brought in young lettuce from his garden, and Faaone had Tiare put it in a salad for supper. Donald, who ate some of it, at once became violently ill. He called it ptomaine poisoning, which he had contracted before. Faaone, alarmed and suspicious, wanted to rush down for some native remedy, but Donald would not let her go. He induced vomiting with the white of eggs and soon felt better.

"It was that salad," he said. "What was in it besides my lettuce?"

"Fresh fruit and a salad dressing of oil and lime juice. It should have been harmless."

"Maybe it was the combination," said Donald, dubiously.

But Faaone did not believe it, and later she gathered some of the lettuce and hurried down to Hing. The old Chinese examined the leaves and found upon them a very fine green powder, almost the same color as the leaf. It did not readily come off.

"Paris green," whispered Hing in Faaone's ear.

"Oh! Donald must have sprayed our lettuce. Don't tell anyone, Hing," she pleaded.

Donald was waiting on the porch, watching the sunset, when she returned.

"Donald, your illness—it was—Paris green," panted Faaone. She had run the last few yards through the darkening jungle.

"What? How in the hell could I eat Paris green?" demanded Donald.

"It's a powder—on our lettuce. I saw it. And Hing told me."

"But how, in God's name, did it get on the lettuce? Who put it there? And *why?*"

"To frighten me. To make you sick, Don—perhaps kill you!"

"Oh, I see. I *am* stupid. I'll take a look out there now, while it's still light enough to see."

While he was gone, Faaone sat on the step trying to still the rage in her breast and to rouse her cunning instead.

"No tracks in the garden," said Donald as he rejoined her. "But outside, toward the trail, I found a footprint made by a big bare foot."

"It has begun," rejoined Faaone.

Donald sensed her seriousness but still could not quite believe the threat was real. The Paris green was a filthy trick, but hardly fatal. "Well, darling," he declared, "we'll just have to outwit them, that's all. You're smarter than any of them. I've got eyes and brains. Or, we could leave them— Let's move across the mountains to Vairao."

125

"Leave my home—my reef? Oh, Donald, I could not live on Tahiti away from here."

"All right, then. To hell with them!"

Faaone echoed that trenchant ejaculation, but she could not emulate his courage. Yet when Donald was asleep she crept out of bed, dressed herself, and, covered with a dark shawl, she left the house. Half the night appeared black, that side toward the mountains being wrapped in a misty cloud. Toward the sea there were shining stars to light the trail, which was so familiar she could have traveled it in pitch darkness. Running from the slightest noise, she kept on through the jungle, until at last she reached the clearing. Lamps burned low in most of the houses, but her mother's house was bright with lights and loud with revelry. Faaone glided among the flowers to peep in a window. The large front room was full of men and women with bottles in their hands and merriment on their lips. Faaone fled on down the trail into the darkness. Many francs had come that way that day.

She went on to the village. At the first house she found Tapo, the crippled fisherman, who was startled at the sight of her. But on recognizing her he asked her in. His women were absent. Naked children stirred on the low bed.

"Tapo, the daughter of Matureo is troubled," said Faaone. "Evil days boded by the tupapa'us are at hand. Are you my friend?"

"Your mother's mother gave me a home when I had no mother."

"Tapo, do you hear talk?"

"My women talk, yes."

"Of what?"

"Of many things. They have seen the tupapa'u with the leper's hands. Some man has made Frangi pregnant. A red light swings in the dusk on the canyon wall above your house. Moto has been drunk. Much money went over Hing's counter this

126

day. Your white father visits Fitieu and drinks. The daughter of—"

"Enough, Tapo. Take this and keep silent."

Faaone glided on down the coast, behind the cottages, with the wet wind threshing her hair and the long shawl flapping around her. The cloud bank was encroaching on the sea, blotting out the stars. She found Punerie alone, brooding over his fire. As she appeared, like an apparition, he leaped to his feet, his hands held out as if to ward off assault.

"Punerie, it is Faaone," she said, loosing the shawl from her head, and parting her disheveled hair from her face.

"Ah-wai! I see—Faaone," he gasped.

"Are you my friend?"

"No. I am the Tahitian who is not good enough for white Faaone to marry."

"Punerie, you are good enough, if I wanted you for a husband. But it is your friendship I seek. Can you be bought with money —much money?"

"No. You know that I cannot, else you would not have come."

"I am in terrible trouble, Punerie. I need a friend."

"There are those in Fitieu who say you cannot find one."

"Make them liars, Punerie," she responded, pleading. "If you help me save him, I will give myself to you—for a day—a night."

"No."

"Would you scorn Faaone?"

"I wanted you for my wife—to lay babies in my arms. I wanted to drive out that white strain—that bastard blood—in you. I wanted you to return to your people and be lost in them, Faaone. As you must in the end!"

"No, Punerie! I never will."

"You will, Faaone. Your reef calls you even now. Your heart is not white."

"Then I come to you in vain, Punerie?"

"What do you want of me?"

"Go to my mother, my sisters. Tell them you hate the Faaone who is lost to you. Tell them at Hing's at the himone. Brag of it in the marketplace at Papeete. Let Benstokes see you are no longer my friend. Curse my white lover to him. Drink with him —accept his money. But watch and listen all the time for the evil that is working to destroy me. Can you do that for me, Punerie?"

"Yes, I can do that. But I cannot see or hear the tupapa'us."

"You can, if you are not afraid."

"Punerie fears no man—no living thing."

"Then be my one friend. I am an outcast. There is no other person I can ask. No brave man . . . Watch Moto. We found his footprint in the trail below our garden."

"Moto is a coward. He and his people all fear your white man because he speared Tavarie."

"They will work in the dark, like tupapa'us."

"Not only for Tavarie's sake," said Punerie, somberly. "If it has begun—"

"It has begun."

"Your mother, your sisters, want Perth killed for their own sakes."

"Yes. And Benstokes wants it for his sake."

"Because he is your father?"

"No, because he wants to be my lover."

Punerie's face twisted suddenly, his expression a strange mixture of fury and grief. His hands clenched. He accepted it as natural that this white man should want his own native daughter, and he hated him for it.

"Faaone, if Benstokes is behind this, I will help you."

"I want to be sure."

"It is done. Punerie is like the moray among fishes."

"Thank you, my friend— I must go now."

"Wait. The storm breaks."

"He will worry. Good night."

Faaone covered her head and went out by the red flare into

the night. The coconut trees were threshing violently. The thunder on the reef vied with an oncoming roar from the mountains. Heavy, scattering raindrops pelted her as she sped across the narrow strip of the road. She passed through the yellow flares from Hing's store on through Fitieu to the stone bridge that marked her trail. Wind and rain roared down the valley to meet her, but she pushed on, feeling her way. Soon the torrent of silver rain gleamed in the lights from her mother's house, and she passed through the clearing into the black jungle. An instinct for direction, long habit on that trail, guided her rightly. The rain soaked through her clothes, chilling her to the bone, and her feet slopped through puddles of water. But her discomfort was nothing, nor her wrath, compared to the fearful sense that there was a shadow stalking her up the trail.

At last, through the leaves she saw the thin, splintered rays of light from her home, and emerging from the jungle ran across the open to the porch.

"Faaone?" called Donald sharply, from within.

"Yes, I am—back."

He looked up to see her standing in the doorway, soaking wet, her usually warm-toned face ashen with terror: "Faaone—" He started up. He wanted to protect her but did not know where the danger lay. He could only take her in his arms. It was a long time before she stopped trembling.

In the days that followed, little things happened—like pin-pricks—exasperating in their apparent triviality, when Faaone anticipated more dire attempts. Thieves stole her garden tools, her long bamboo with the hook on the end to cut down breadfruits, her coconuts—anything left outdoors. Punerie sent word by Tupa that her canoe had been set adrift on an ebb tide. Tiare came one morning with her plump cheeks tear-stained. She had been beaten because she persisted in working for Faaone. Frangi had not been near her for days. Tupa brought word she was sick, but Faaone knew what it was that kept her away.

One day Tupa, who had been running errands and helping

Donald at odd jobs, did not put in an appearance. Faaone went to see his mother, her eldest sister. Ena, broad-faced and placid, assured Faaone that Tupa had been ordered to attend the district school. Faaone told her sister that this need not keep Tupa from helping her, but Ena said she needed the boy herself.

"I will pay for Tupa—one dollar a week," Faaone offered.

"Sister, my boy is not for hire."

"No, Ena, but *you* are," retorted Faaone. There was evidence on Ena's person and around the house of recent prosperity.

Faaone left with a sense of being slowly walled-in, shut away from her family and old friends. Before the week was out, Hing had refused to give her credit. When she paid, he was evasive and imperturbable, but made it clear he could not serve her any more. She was driven to buy supplies in Tautira, the largest village on that coast of the island. There were several stores, but the distance was too far to walk with burdens. She had to resort to her long unused bicycle. When that was stolen she was at a loss to know what to do, and she had to tell Donald.

There had been a time when Donald would have advised Faaone simply to get rid of him, but that was past. He could not leave her now. He swore like a white man and said he would go to Tautira after the groceries.

"But, Don, I am afraid. It is not safe," she said.

"In the daytime? When your people just melt into the green whenever they see me? If you're worried, I'll carry a spear."

"Darling, you must not kill another native. You would go to jail. Then what would become of me?"

"At least the pressure would be off you then."

"I'd rather have the pressure and you, Don, whatever else may happen!"

The slow-coming catastrophe brought out Faaone's native qualities. She must meet cunning with cunning. Hatred, which had softened with Donald's love, burst out again, directed at those enemies who worked in the dark. She had not been out on the reef since Donald had come to her, but had often gone up the river to the bathing pool where he had first seen her; now she resorted to the pool nearby. She feared now to take Donald up the streams to fish for nato. Their activities were confined to the clearing and frequent trips to Tautira.

"Faa, what do you know about this?" asked Donald one day, coming in with that blue flame in his eyes. "You know that hideous fellow with one leg bigger than his body—he has to crawl, dragging it after him?"

"Yes. Toietu. The man with fefe. What of him?"

"Well, he has put up his hut on our brook, on the trail not a hundred steps from the clearing. Surely he had help. And he's squatting there now, with coconuts and pigs and chickens."

Faaone's comment was English profanity. Donald laughed. But Faaone's face was somber.

"Don, he wants you to get sick. He wants you to catch it."

"He? You don't mean Toietu."

"No. I mean Benstokes. Don, I have not wanted you to know, but it has got to come out. I am sure he is at the bottom of much of this persecution."

"That filthy drunk!" Donald spat. "Faa, did you know he had the—the gall to make a play for Winifred?"

"That took gall, all right—but from what I gather it wasn't hopeless," retorted Faaone, stung to sarcasm by this unexpected reaction to her fears. Was Winifred still so much on his mind, then?

"What? Oh, hell!" he exclaimed, and flushed a painful red. After a moment he resumed: "But—I don't get this at all. Your suspicion that Bennet-Stokes is behind all these things, especially this fefe man—it's just ridiculous. If it were so—by God . . ."

"I may be wrong, Donald," interrupted Faaone, hastily, "that is, about Benstokes. But somebody is bent on sickening you with me and this life here." She had not seen that hard expression on his face before. If she were not very clever she would have her lover adding to their calamity, and perhaps making a tragedy of it. He seemed marked for tragedy.

"That can't be done, darling. I love you more than anyone I ever knew. And I'm happy, except when . . ."

"I know, darling," replied Faaone. "But this must end. You could catch fefe."

"Me? Nonsense. Mosquitoes don't bite me. So elephantiasis is out, as far as I'm concerned. Anyway it's not bad in its first stages, for a white man."

"My handsome Donald!" she cried, suddenly envisioning him with the deformity. She shuddered. "You see, Don, I am white. I cannot stand the thought of fefe for you."

"So it's my masculine beauty you fell for?" he replied facetiously, bringing a reluctant smile to her lips. "Seriously, honey, I can't possibly get fefe, so moving in old Toietu was wasted effort. But I'd be an ass if I ignored all this. I'm getting as suspicious as a kicked pup."

"All I beg of you is to do what I tell you," she replied earnestly. "Whatever all this means, I promise you, I'll be clever enough to avert it."

From that day Donald appeared to change gradually, becoming watchful and brooding, where formerly he had idled and dreamed the hours away. He was more attentive and loving than ever to Faaone, helped her in all her tasks, seldom left her alone, and developed a sensitiveness to the sounds of the lonely nights. They cut a trail around Toietu's hut, so they could pass without seeing him. They heard him at night, though, drinking and carousing with his friends. Faaone did not need to ask who supplied the bottles.

Days passed, and each one bore down more oppressively on Faaone, for even happenings that might have been natural she could not accept as such. The days, however, were as nothing to endure compared to the nights. Wrapped in Donald's arms, sure of his protection and love, Faaone still could not be free from dread, from the awful nameless menace that hovered in the darkness. Of what did all her stubborn passion, her sacrifice of the money and luxuries she had become used to, her risk—perhaps, even of life itself—avail her? She knew these subtle Tahitians. They had been changed only outwardly and fettered by the white men. Egged on by smooth tongues, plied with money and drink, they would perform any hellish task.

In the dead of night if she was not awakened by mysterious sounds, then Donald would be. He had ceased to laugh at her and tease her about her tupapa'us.

"What are they, darling?" he whispered one night, holding her close. "Ghosts? Spirits? Specters? Or just fears?"

"Nobody knows. But they *are*. I have seen them. And they are around now."

"Well, if they take us we'll be together."

"*They* won't take us. They just foretell an awful fate. Like a dog baying at night to announce that death is near."

"Faaone, my Reef Girl—" He began to caress her gently, but she was still stiff with fear.

"Listen! Don, do you hear that step?"

"No. To hell with steps on my trail. I've heard them for years. Faaone—" He held her close with one hand while the other traced a long, slow curve down her back. "You are my Tahitian sunrise and sunset, my day and night. My dream of beauty come true. . . . Oh, God, how I love you! The past is dead. The future means only you—all the long hot golden days—all the dark nights like this—only you!"

"Be still, my lover," she whispered and held him to her.

The next afternoon, while Faaone was making a rare salad of heart of palm, something Donald had not tasted, he came staggering to her in the kitchen, ghost-white, with lightning in his eyes and his blood-soaked shirt held to his temple.

"Donald!"

"I've been shot. It's not serious," he said hoarsely. "Just a scratch, really. But it's bleeding like hell—get some linen."

Mute, with contracting heart, Faaone ran to comply. She came back to find him sitting on a chair with his head bent and blood dripping on the floor. She washed off the blood and, folding a pad over the shallow groove, bound it tightly with a bandage.

"Where—were you?" She was determined to be calm.

"Up the fei trail," he replied. "I wanted oranges, and I had to go farther than usual. It happened when I was coming back. I didn't hear the shot, but felt a blow. It knocked me flat."

"Did you see anyone—or hear anyone?"

"I didn't *see* anything but wild chickens flying. But I did hear other shots. It might have been villagers hunting on that big flat. Probably it was an accident—if someone meant to murder me he'd have ambushed the trail and blown my brains out."

"No. Natives do not kill a white man so. Remember the Tahitians are captives of the French government. They can murder one another, and the French care not at all, but seldom if ever do natives kill a white. If they do they leave no trace."

"Faaone, if I *did* know I had been shot at by some bloody devil, would that help matters?"

"Yes, it would."

But though he importuned Faaone to tell him how or why she would not answer. It began to dawn upon her that meeting Donald's enemies with their own weapons—stealth and deceit —would not be enough. Moto, or another of Tavarie's kin, certainly would have killed Donald long ago except for fear of him and fear of the French government's quick punishment of any violence done to a white. Bennet-Stokes plotted to get rid of Donald one way or another, but it seemed to her that he had also stooped to low native craft. No, they were not trying to kill him, but to make it impossible for her and Donald to live in that district, or any other in Tahiti.

"Don, would you go away with me, if I had to do that to save you?"

134

"Leave Tahiti? You couldn't. You'd be like a fish out of water. You'd be like a bird of paradise without green jungle and fruit and golden waters."

"Yes. But lately I've felt driven. Could we go, Donald?"

"I would have no choice. If you wanted to go, I could only follow you, Faaone. But I know you couldn't leave here. Cheer up, darling. We have each other, and we'll beat them yet."

"But things must grow worse before they ever get better. Even now, we live from hand to mouth. We are surrounded by pigs. Pigs under every palm! Filth and stink! We cannot even keep a garden to work in. What will the worse be? I am at the end of my rope, as you white people say. I have been waiting, waiting, waiting. . . ."

"For what?"

"To find out *who!* Punerie was to find out for me—everything. But he might betray me."

"Punerie? I don't believe it. He still loves you, and if he can will help you—and me, for your sake."

The next day dawned without the usual glory. A storm threatened—not one of the hourly swoopings of a rain-soaked cloud, but a dense black mass that hid the peaks and sent ropes of white fire down into the purple canyons. Out over the lagoon and sea an ominous calm prevailed, and a moaning that was neither reef nor wind sounded on the sultry air.

"It's the full-moon storm," said Donald, as he stood and watched the lightning play on the mountain slopes behind the house.

"It might be the hurricane that is coming," replied Faaone.

"Why do you say that?"

"Because it is time Tahiti had another. The rainy season is here. And yesterday I heard that Rangiroa has not seen the sun for ten days. It is hurricane weather."

"I'd like to see one."

"Do not wish more danger upon us. Let us go in, Don. The lightning frightens me."

"You go, Faaone. I want to watch the storm come down the valley."

Faaone went into the kitchen, but despite her activities she could not entirely shut out the elements. From one window she saw the light of day darken and a canopy of copper cloud stretch out over the lagoon. Off to the north, in the direction of the atoll Tetiaroa, a murky, sulphurous sky lowered to the gloomy sea. White water showed around the headland beyond Tautira. The waves came swiftly, rolling long and high. A dark ripple began to ridge the lagoon.

From the other window Faaone saw a storm spectacle up the valley that supported her uneasy expectations. No gray pall of rain bore down upon the green; no trailing veils hung from the dense black roof. But streaks of lightning shot out of the clouds, and ripping peals of thunder followed. The one rocky stretch of the river appeared to dance with balls of fire. Intermittent gusts of wind threshed the palms, and huge scattering drops of rain splashed the pool and spattered on the roof. An unnatural dusk had fallen.

Donald's thumping leap upon the porch brought Faaone erect and thrilling. He ran towards her, his hair ruffled, his eyes like dark holes in a sheet.

"Faa, am I drunk—or insane?" he cried. "So help me, God, I *saw* one of them."

"One of what?"

"Your tupapa'us. I was out there listening—looking. It was all so strange—like thin smoke, the veil or haze that came down the valley. Smelled like sulphur. The lightning was cracking brimstone up on the peaks. All of a sudden a transparent wave of darkness swept down, like wind. I began to feel odd. All the flowers from our flambuoyant tree went flying on the wind—a red flame. I saw fire run down the waterfall. I saw something like jack-o'-lanterns hanging over the river. Then—" he stopped to catch his breath.

"What *else* did you see?" Faaone shook him, wildly.

"By heaven! it was neither human nor natural. This thing came right out of the gloom of the jungle. It didn't walk—it didn't have any feet. It was shaped like a bat—a huge bat! No! More like a shield, such as the Africans fight with. It had no color, but it was dark. I could see through it. Long black thin arms in sleeves—with white things like loose gloves over skeleton hands . . . Faaone, I *saw* this—this *thing.* I watched it a whole endless moment. It can't have been a hallucination."

"No. It was no hallucination. It was a tupapa'u." Faaone's words were measured, her voice deadly calm. She was cold to the marrow of her bones. "Donald, I must heed this warning. I must go to mother."

"What good will that do?"

"She'll *tell* me. Donald, we cannot fight longer with white intelligence and courage. I am a Tahitian. All this is punishment for my having denied my blood. Stay here, Donald. I shall find out how to save us."

Faaone ran out of the house and flew across the clearing to the jungle trail. Myriad leaves swooped by on the wind. The palms gave forth a whistling sound, and the heavy nuts were dropping all around her. Long green banana leaves were ripped into fluttering fringe. She gained the river clearing and fled along the open like one pursued, on past the closed and silent huts to her mother's house.

Across the porch white hibiscus and frangipani blossoms blew, drifting over the floor. Faaone opened the door and rushed in. A brood of children huddled around her mother in a corner. Matureo cried out at sight of Faaone, "Aue! Aue!"

"Mother, it is the hurricane."

"Yes, my daughter."

"But we are safe under the mountain."

"There is the river and the sea."

"If they rise you can carry your things out. My house is high under the hill. Mother, it is not the hurricane that frightens me."

And breathlessly Faaone repeated to Matureo what Donald had told her about the coming of the bat tupapa'us.

"Mother, he always laughed at me, my white man. He did not believe in tupapa'us. Day after day and night after night the curse laid upon Donald by you and Benstokes and the ghost of Tavarie worked upon us with theft and hate and hunger, with footsteps in the dark of night and gun shots by day, with that hideous Toietu lying naked in his cloud of mosquitoes. And my Donald laughed and scorned the things I feared and held me to his breast in the night. Until today he never believed. But he saw this one—Mother, what does it mean?"

"Death!" intoned Matureo.

"For me?"

"For your white man. For anyone who sees it."

"What can I do to save him?"

"It is too late! Unless you give him up—and then, maybe too late!"

"Matureo, I will send him away. I will make friends with Moto. I will go to Benstokes. You will be rich again."

"Ah-wai! Then at last Faaone loves a white man!" exclaimed the woman.

"Yes, yes. I love Donald. I began in hate—the old hate. But now . . . I must save him from this curse of Tahiti. *Your* blood in me, mother, does not curdle at the thought of Benstokes's arms. But I am half-white. And with all I am I love—I love Donald! Now I must drain out my white blood! My own father!"

She burst into a storm of weeping and, falling upon her knees, put her head in her mother's lap. Matureo stroked her hair, but her face was like a graven image, without hope. After a long while, she spoke.

"Faaone, I cannot help you. But I can tell you something that may make what you must do a little easier to bear. Benstokes is not your father."

"Matureo!" Faaone turned her tear-stained face up, staring at the older woman in disbelief.

"It is true, my daughter. I had an American lover once. I loved him as you love Donald, but for a few weeks only. Benstokes never knew. He had been away, and later I deceived him about my time. He thinks you are his own flesh and blood."

"But *why*, Mother?"

"He would have killed us both, I think, if he had known. Besides," she shrugged, "I wanted what he could give us both —this house, your education. Now, he wants you, Faaone, as all men want you. And more. He wants to take you away to the great cities of the world—to deck you in pearls and diamonds and rich gowns—to show you off to envious men—to take you to London and make you a queen in the moving pictures."

"So—Faaone means so much to him!" Faaone was calmer now and cold as ice.

"Benstokes is a devil of jealousy. Your living with Donald has turned him until he is on fire with hate. Unless you go to him, death will not be enough to visit upon your white man. He will destroy. He will make Donald something that you must loathe."

"Ah!" Faaone leaped to her feet. The fury of the blood in her ears drowned the roar of the wind, but her voice was deadly calm. "Thank you, my mother, for the truth. And be at peace. Save yourself and the little ones from the storm. If you lose your house I will build you another. I go to Benstokes."

She ran out again, drawing her shawl over her head. Darkness now filled the valley, and the gale almost lifted her off her feet. She made for the village. From the void bellowed the terrible voices of the reef in fury. Rain did not fall, it blew straight at her, stinging like thrown pebbles.

"Like Toietu!" hissed Faaone through her teeth. "Donald, my beautiful boy, with his clean white limbs! Cursed by my father who was not my father—who would kill by fefe! Benstokes, I see you now with my white mind, but I shall deal with you as if I were born all brown from Matureo's womb."

She made her way to the beach, watchful of the falling coconuts and leaves. It was almost dark in the grove. A black surge with frothy crest ran up the shore, lapping around the tree trunks. Faaone passed one dimly lighted hut after another until she came to Punerie's.

In the subdued lamp-flare, his blanched face and distended eyes checked the greeting on her lips.

"*Faaone!*"

"Punerie, the hurricane comes. Your mother and sisters?"

"They have just left. We must all take to high ground. What are you doing here?"

"Have you failed me, Punerie?"

"No, Faaone. Punerie has kept his word."

"So long! Day after day, and this curse creeping—creeping like a scorpion."

"Faaone, I was just coming to find you."

"You would have come tonight?"

"Tonight, Faaone. I have learned all you wanted to know. All our people think and say and do. Why they have failed you."

"Benstokes!"

"Yes, Faaone. Whatever you and your Donald Perth have feared and suffered is the work of the Englishman."

"I knew. All the time I knew! But I must have proof. Proof, Punerie, else I cannot kill him."

"*Faaone!* You must not kill him," ejaculated Punerie, seizing her by the shoulders. "He is white. You know the French, that we are dirt under their feet."

But Faaone did not answer this. She said only, "Talk—and louder. The wind grows strong."

"These thatch walls have ears. There are tupapa'us about."

"One proof, Punerie. The rest can wait."

Punerie gazed fearfully about his shadowy hut and out the door into the shaft of yellow light. Faaone saw his brawny throat contract as he swallowed hard. He put his lips to her ear.

"Moto has been here. He just left."

"Moto!"

"Yes." She saw him tremble. "I made friends with Moto. Got drunk with him. Lay with his women. He trusted me. He believed, as they all believe, that I hate Faaone. . . . Aue! So easy for a soft-footed native! Moto had been to your house once, twice—looked in at your window. He saw you asleep. He saw your man asleep beside you, close under the window. . . . He has taken money—thousands of francs—from Benstokes. He meant to do it tonight. So easy. Just one quick jab in at your window. You would not awake. Even Donald Perth might sleep on. But if he did awaken—too late!"

"But what does he plan to *do,* Punerie? *Kill* him?"

"Worse!"

Punerie's dark fingers closed with a plunging motion. "He carries a needle, what the whites call a dope needle. He will stick your Donald Perth with it, and he will sicken and become foul before he dies."

"What—what is in this needle?" The words seemed to stick in Faaone's throat.

Close to her ear Punerie whispered. She recoiled at what she heard.

"Punerie—I—I didn't hear."

His lips moved again: "Leprosy!"

The word might have been burning poison shot through her blood. God's mercy—no! All that was white in her revolted at this hideous and unsupportable lie. It must be a lie! But Punerie leaned back, his heavy hands on her shoulders, his bronze face gleaming in the yellow light, his black eyes clear and true.

"Yes, Faaone. I have seen it. Moto was on his way to your house tonight, but the hurricane brought night before its hour. In a lightning flash he saw something behind him. He turned back. A brighter flash showed him a tupapa'u. He made for my home. Every time the light flashed the tupapa'u was closer. It

141

had no feet, he said. It was like half of a canoe upside down. It swung two paddles, like arms. It had white hands that flapped in the wind. . . . Moto was afraid. He told me how Benstokes bribed a man at the leper colony—one with some medical training. He procured the needle and poured something over the skin ulcer of a leper and caught the drippings in the needle. The leper thought he was receiving a treatment that would make the skin sore heal. Moto showed me the needle. He begged me to take it. He gave me money—see, here it is. At first I refused. Then I pretended I would do it, to get the package away from him. He gave it to me, but suddenly he snatched it back and shrieked, 'I must do it, I must do it!' He fled as if the devil were at his heels."

A glittering flash of lightning showed the steely rain, the threshing palms, the frothy surge beating up the beach. Their clamor echoed in Faaone's bursting heart. Now the native in her crowded out the gifts and teachings of the whites. She was a tigress at bay. She was Faaone, of Tahiti.

"Punerie, lend me your knife."

The man's dark hand moved toward his belt. It shook as he held the gleaming blade out to Faaone.

"Faaone, I will go—with you," he whispered.

"No, Punerie. This is for me."

11

❋

❋

❋

Fear of the hurricane did not abide in Donald Perth, although he still had an incomprehensible fear of the sea and Faaone's tupapa'us had become dreadful realities—he was no longer able to explain away with his white man's reason the mystery of the native spirits. But his great fear was that he seemed destined to lose Faaone, who had become more than his life to him. She had returned from her mad excursion to the village at the height of the storm, her shawl and pareu torn. Her face was white and set, and she had refused to answer his questions. She clung to him, but her body would not be warmed, and despite her nearness she was, he sensed, far away from him. He thought that in the morning she would leave him, and he was afraid she would not come back.

So he lay wide-eyed in the blackness of the night, with Faaone in his arms, listening to the hollow roar and piercing shriek of the storm. When it lulled momentarily, the sullen chafing sound of the flooded river and the din of the surf filled his ears.

Faaone—too—lay awake, clinging to him silently, but aloof, locked in her native fatalism. The hurricane, like the tupapa'us, was a visitation from the angry gods of a race who had taken aliens to their hearts. Donald yearned to penetrate that closed region of her thought, for it was the primitive in her—the animal grace and beauty, the unabatable passion—that possessed him utterly. In this life they were now living it seemed that both his white heritage and her education were out of place.

The sound of the wind grew louder and higher in pitch as its velocity steadily increased. Large limbs were stripped from trees and hurled through the night against what were probably some native huts. Faaone's little palm-thatched house was nestled under a protecting overhang of cliff; still, smaller objects whipped against the shuttered windows with a sound like the cracking of a bullwhip.

Faaone trembled, and he drew her still more closely to him. He realized he did not care if they were carried away by flood or wind, as long as—if he had to die—it was with her in his arms. But with the coming of dawn, the hurricane vanished, much more quickly than it had appeared, leaving the house, its surroundings and its occupants spent but largely intact.

Faaone arose and dressed, and presently she called Donald to breakfast. Her warmth and color had not returned, and her strained face appeared incapable of a smile.

"Donald, I am going into Papeete today," she announced after he had eaten.

"But what about the road? Will it be open so soon?"

"If it is not, I will wait. But I must go, as soon as possible." Her voice was low, with an ominous finality that brooked no argument.

"If it is open, I will go with you," he rejoined.

"No, not this time. I have to go alone."

"But *why*, Faaone?"

"We have been made poor. I must sell my pearls. I will not be gone long."

Though he knew that she was lying, there was something in her mood that forbade him to pursue the matter.

Faaone went back into the house and reappeared a few minutes later, carrying her red, wide-brimmed, white-banded hat and her grass satchel, which he saw contained her red shoes and some other articles. Her shapely legs were bare, and she had on sneakers. She was prepared to wade through water and mud. Still somber and composed, she bade Donald goodbye. He did not reveal to her the formless dread that had settled over him.

"Faaone, ask for my mail at the post office, . . . and, please darling, come home quickly."

After she was gone, he went to work to clear away the bread-fruit leaves that had blown in piles upon the porch. Then he did the chores. The day was nearly done by the time he had finished. She had not returned, so he surmised that the road was passable. He made a simple supper and went to bed early.

The next morning he made his way down the trail to see what destruction the hurricane had left.

Toietu was gone, and so was his shack. Below that, in the clearing, palm-thatched huts were flat on the ground, which was littered with coconuts. Small boys were gathering them in piles. The river had encroached to the edge of the clearing, but Matureo's house and those adjacent were uninjured. The hibiscus bushes and frangipani trees had been stripped of blossoms. Donald saw few people, except the children, and concluded they had gone to the village, where the damage would be greater.

The lagoon still resembled a muddy, swirling lake, and an angry though subsiding sea beat on the reef. Some of the cane houses along the shore, notably Punerie's, had withstood the ravages of wind and waves, but many were in ruins. The village cottages and store and himone houses, however, still stood. Built of wood and tin-roofed, evidently they had not born the brunt of the storm. Up and down the road, the hedges drooped without a flower.

Donald went up to Hing's, indifferent to the stares of the villagers gathered there. What few scraps of talk he caught corroborated his conviction that Fitieu and the north side of the main island had escaped the worst of the storm. As he was leaving, he encountered Punerie, whose somber face lost its rigidity for an instant in greeting.

"Anyone drowned?" asked Donald.

"Not in our district. We are cut off from Tautira, but the road to Papeete was not washed out. The storm was not nearly as strong on that side. The bus stayed here night before last." Punerie averted his bronze face and clasped and unclasped his big hands, making his knuckles show white. "We found Moto in the road yesterday. He was dead!"

"Moto? My God! Did you tell Faaone? She left yesterday for Papeete."

"Matureo was here in the himone, lamenting with Moto's family. Faaone surely heard. She sat in the bus by Hing's. It was almost noon before it left."

"What happened to him?"

"I do not know. Some boys found him. He had been stabbed, but surely not to death—scratched merely. He was the color of ashes."

"Struck by lightning?"

"No!" cried Punerie, with a violent gesture. "Donald— Did Faaone tell you about—about Moto?"

"Punerie, she told me nothing."

"You must ask her."

Something in the man's voice shook Donald. He leaned forward to grasp Punerie's arm.

"Punerie, you know something—what is it?" he cried hoarsely.

"No, no, let me go! She made me promise not to tell anyone."

"Remember, you loved her once, as I do now. You must tell me."

Punerie looked at him, long and searchingly. Finally he spoke. "Yes, Donald Perth, you do love her as I once did, as no white man has before. I will tell you the story of Moto."

Donald's face turned ashen as Punerie talked.

"So it is Benstokes who has been behind it all—the stealing, the bribing of Toietu, the shots. She hinted as much once, but I did not really believe her, and she did not seem sure. All of that because of me. . . ."

"No, my friend, not just because of you. Benstokes wants her, and you are in the way. She has gone to him now, to save you. I could not stop her."

"But I will stop her—and him. Thank you, my brother." Donald held out his hand. "Perhaps you have saved us both."

"Go quickly—before it is too late."

Donald ran back to Faaone's house. Among his possessions was a long slim knife with a scabbard. He had used it primarily to clean fish. After changing his clothes, he carefully hid the scabbard and knife underneath his shirt. He also took what was left of the money in Faaone's drawer. Then he ran back toward the road.

Luckily, the Papeete bus had not left, and he found a seat among the natives, with baskets full of wind-felled fruit and produce destined for the Papeete market. This morning he found little comfort in the singing of the Tahitians or the beauty of the magnificent sun-drenched reef and sky. He was brought out of his morbid reverie only once on the long trip, when the bus rolled to a stop on the left side of the road by a high white-washed fence. Isolated behind it were a number of frame buildings that appeared to face the sea apprehensively. No passengers boarded the bus here, nor was anything put on. Some fruit and fish were taken off, and that was all.

"What is this place?" Donald asked his fellow passengers, who gazed at the buildings with a mixture of fear and disgust.

One who spoke a little English said, "Very bad—very sick people here— white man's disease—they call it lep-ro-sy."

Donald peered over the fence. So this was the dreaded leper colony of Tahiti. He saw a number of natives lying and sitting on the porches, all motionless. Some fixed expressionless eyes upon the crowd in the bus. Gaunt, dark faces, wasted bodies,

147

unwholesome skins, attested in some degree to their fatal malady. He noticed one in particular, whose face was covered, and from whose short-sleeved shirt protruded skinny wrists and hands, the color of gray ashes. There were no fingers on the hands. He drew back from the window, consumed by pity and horror. But for Faaone, this might have been his fate.

As it was just before noon when the bus arrived, Donald made his way to the Cercle Bougainville, where he would be likely to find the local businessmen and tourists, perhaps even Bennet-Stokes himself.

There were mostly strange faces in the club. He found an empty table and sat down. The rum drink he ordered was warm and heady, and he quickly finished it and ordered another. Suddenly a hand clapped him on the back. It was Bellair, visibly taken back at seeing him.

"Donald Perth, by all that's holy. How are you? You're looking fit and well. The last I heard, you'd gone native to live with those queer nature men at the end of the island."

Donald grasped the offered hand. "It's good to see you again, Bell. Yes, I'm well but not with them any more. I couldn't stand them for very long. Sit down and have a drink."

"We missed you—particularly after your lovely Winifred went home." Neither he nor Donald mentioned the reason for her going, or the death of Tavarie.

"I've been living out near Tautira for some months now," Donald said. "It's nice to come back and see old friends."

"I seem to remember Faaone was from Tautira. We never see her around any more. Do you see her at all?"

"Occasionally, but I'm really somewhat of a hermit. Live by myself, you know." Donald gave Bellair a keen glance, but the older man seemed unaware of the deception. If he knew any more, his face did not show it.

"Have you seen Bennet-Stokes around lately?" queried Donald, trying desperately to sound casual.

"Yes, as a matter of fact, I did—last night he came in here.

148

Looked bad. Then just this morning I heard they took him to the hospital. I don't know what was wrong with him, perhaps too much to drink. He's quite a boozer, you know."

Abruptly, Donald stood up. "Well, thanks, Bell. It's good to see you, but I have to run along. I'll drop by later."

Bellair gave him a startled look. "Well, we can talk some other time. See you later," he added, regretfully.

Donald shook his hand and left, stopping just long enough to drop a bill on the table. Only one thought pervaded his mind —he must find Faaone. Perhaps she was already on the bus back to Tautira. He looked at his watch. There was time, if he hurried.

The bus station was crowded, but there was no sign of Faaone. He spent several hours searching the hotels and crisscrossing the streets of Papeete, but to no avail. Then he had an inspiration, though the thought almost sickened him. Kelly's Bar—the worst, most notorious dive in the South Seas. Could she have gone there?

It was dark inside, the clink of glasses mingling with jukebox music and the sound of muffled voices. Several of the slim, bare-armed, sharp-eyed girls eyed him provocatively as he went from table to table, but he ignored their overtures. Then he saw Faaone, at a booth in the far end of the room, sitting alone with her head lowered in her arms.

"Faaone, thank God I found you!"

She stared up at him dully. He could see that she was drunk.

"Well, Donald, my high-class white lover, come and have a drink with your Tahitian whore."

"Faaone, I've come to take you home."

"Home—where is that? I have no home, except here!"

He sat down opposite her, and grasped her hands in his. "Faaone, my darling, I love you. Punerie told me everything. I know what brought you to Papeete—to Bennet-Stokes—last night. I came here to kill him, if necessary."

She looked at him uncomprehendingly and tried to pull

149

away. "What do you mean? I went to Benstokes yesterday. I danced naked in front of him. I let him fondle me—have his way with me. And then when he was drunk and asleep, I . . ." her voice trailed off. "How can you ever love me again? You are a white man. I am just a Tahitian whore. Go away and leave me alone."

"Faaone, it's over. I don't care what you did. It really doesn't matter. You're mine, and I've come to take you home."

"All right, lover boy. Just so you know what you have."

He helped her to her feet. She clung to him, all of a sudden reduced to tears.

"Do you have anything with you?"

"Oh yes, my satchel, I cannot forget my satchel. Under the table—hidden, you see, so Benstokes cannot . . . One hundred thousand francs. It is mine—a gift from my lover." She laughed bitterly, even as tears flowed down her cheeks. "Cannot forget my satchel." He left it where it lay.

As they staggered along past tables whose occupants turned to stare, she said loudly, "This will give some of these fathead Frenchmen something to talk about. Donald Perth in love with Tahiti's most famous whore."

Donald was flushed, but he said nothing. Luckily a taxi was standing just outside the door.

"Let us not go home just yet," she implored. "I do not want anyone there to see me like this."

He directed the driver to the Blue Lagoon, a resort hotel with separate cottages just outside town. While Faaone waited in the cab, he secured a room well away from the road.

Once inside, she collapsed on the bed and gave way to uncontrollable sobs. "Oh Donald, it has been so ghastly. Can you ever forgive me?"

He held her shaking body in his arms. "Darling, it's over. There's nothing to forgive. Whatever you did you did for me. I told you I was prepared to kill him myself." He showed her

150

the knife still in its leather scabbard. "It's all over and we're safe, and . . ." He hesitated, then went on. "I want you for my wife as soon as possible."

She drew back and stared at him. "You would *marry* me? Now? But why? To *save* me?"

He shook her by the shoulders. "No, you fool, to love you! For a long while you took care of me and loved me. Now it is my turn to take care of you. The dark side in me came out with Tavarie. Perhaps the same side of you made you want to revenge yourself against your father."

"But he is not my father, Donald. Even Punerie did not know that. My mother told me. My father was an American—like you."

"I'm glad, for your sake. But it makes no difference to me, my darling—or to our unborn child."

She stared at him. "You know that? How did you find out?"

"Oh, you somehow began to look different—more rounded and more beautiful than ever. . . . And—I think you've missed two months now."

Some of her old spirit seemed to return. "So my white malahine is no longer a boy but a man, with the power to read a woman's mind." She reached out and touched his face lightly.

He kissed her. "Now we are free, you will show me—us," he touched her body, "your world—our world—of the reef," he said softly. "And then I will show you mine. But first you must get some rest."

She sank back in the bed and was soon fast asleep. Donald went out quietly down the cottage steps, for a brief walk. Somehow, despite the terrifying happenings of the past few days, his mind was singularly at ease. Gone was the dread that had haunted him for weeks. As he walked out on the short pier in front of the hotel, the sun was just making resplendent the gold-tipped clouds hovering over Moorea. He thought sadly of Winifred, whose dream of Tahiti had turned into a nightmare.

But all that seemed light years away from him now. He must get Faaone home. In her own surroundings she could become her old self again.

She was still sleeping when he returned, well after dark, nor did she awaken when he slipped into bed beside her.

In the morning they slept late. Faaone was solemn-eyed when she awoke, and Donald was not sure what she remembered of the afternoon before.

He decided to take a taxi home. She was quiet on the ride out, and hung heavily on his arm when they finally went up the trail towards the house.

"Darling, see, Toietu is gone," said Donald, as they passed the squalid clearing where the victim of fefe had lived.

"That hurricane was from God," she answered.

It was still light enough to see when they reached home. Faaone sank down on the porch step and peered up the valley with pensive eyes.

"I should scold you for drinking so much," he began, almost as if to make conversation.

"Beat me, Don," she replied, with her first wan smile.

"Faaone, I wouldn't lay a hand on you. Surely you know that!" he protested.

"Yes, I know that." Suddenly her eyes filled with tears.

"Donald Perth, no white woman could ever have been so true to you as I have been—or done what I have done and been forgiven. I never loved you, but I love you now, with all my native heart—with all my white mind. Perhaps it is ended, our trouble. But don't ask me why, how, or anything."

She fell against him in utter weariness. He gathered her up and carried her in to put her down on the bed, where she was asleep before he had got her undressed.

Faaone slept until the middle of the following afternoon. She awakened, singing a native song. Donald heard her and ran in. She lay half-naked in the pareu he had tried to get on her—languid, hollow-eyed, pale as a tiare-tahiti flower, and as lovely.

She bathed in the pool, donned a blue and white pareu, and, with much of the havoc vanished, presented herself to Donald in the kitchen, where he was getting supper. She embraced him with a serious sweetness that suited the change in her.

Days passed and things seemed to be returning to normal—although some things had changed, as Donald soon noticed. Faaone's mother and sisters began to make overtures with fruit and leis and gifts of fish. Tupa and Tiare returned to their former relations, making Faaone's home their home. Frangi came, too, shyly, draped in a loose pareu. To effect a reconciliation Matureo came, as Faaone had predicted, begging on her knees. Faaone's sisters followed suit, and presently the family was united. The source of discord and resentment had dried up. Even Hing waylaid Faaone on the road, and in Donald's presence won her back to friendliness.

But Faaone puzzled him. There was no mention of his offer to marry her or of the revelation about the baby. Perhaps she had not remembered.

Finally, after several days, he felt he could wait no longer. "Faaone, sit beside me on the bed." He drew her down. "Do you remember what we talked about that night at the Blue Lagoon, just before we came home?"

She looked away, over the valley toward the cloud-shrouded peaks in the distance. Her face was pale.

"Yes, I remember—but I did not believe you meant it," her voice was flat and strained.

"I did my darling. I meant every word. I want you to marry me, as soon as possible."

"Donald, can we not leave things as they are—just you and me and our home here?"

"And what about the baby?"

"I was lying. There is no baby." Her voice was harsh.

Donald laid a hand gently below her breasts. "I know it's there—and you do too."

"How do you know it is even yours?"

"I know. There has only been one time—with Bennet-Stokes —and you were pregnant then. I would stake my life on that."

Her eyes suddenly filled with tears and she clung to him. "Donald, you are far too good for me. I—I don't deserve it."

"Promise me that you'll think about it, won't you?"

She murmured assent. That night their love-making was more passionate and fulfilling than they had known for many weeks. But she made no answer to his proposal.

12

✳

✳

✳

Donald was out on the barrier reef with Faaone for the first time. It was morning, not yet late enough for the roseate columnar clouds to merge with the pearl mass and bank against the peaks, there to condense and darken for the daily rains. The sun was halfway up, hot, though not burning. And a dazzling white light beat upon the azure sea.

This outer coral reef lay a mile or more from the shore across the mosaic of lagoon. It was a reef unlike any of the others he had studied, and, at low tide, vastly different from the savage and restless points on the windward side of the island. The swells, rising lazily out of the blue and moving with stately and varied forms toward the barrier, astounded him with their grandeur and immensity.

Faaone had run the point of her canoe against the ragged coral on the inside of the reef. Donald, absorbed in the coral heads, all gold and purple and bronze, had not looked up to see the surf until Faaone said: "My reef! I might have been born on it, lover. Every day for five years when I was little I came here with the fishermen. I remember when Noturea threw me in. 'Swim or drown, white tomaru!' he said. He was an early lover of Matureo's. He wanted me to drown. But I swam."

"Where did he throw you in?" queried Donald, incredulously.

"I'll show you, in a little while. Let's wade first. Fetch the basket and spear."

The reef was perhaps two hundred feet wide, slightly higher in the center, a russet and bronze color, bare in some parts, covered with seaweeds in others. The six inches of water were alive with fish of endless variety, crabs and morays, starfish and octopuses, sea slugs and sea nettles, and many creatures Donald could not name. Every loose slab of coral had a cowrie shell underneath it, most a brilliant, spotted brown. The swell lapped up over the outer edge of the reef with a melodious roar, crashed to white foam, and spread in a long shallow ripple over the water. Following the first long, wandering line of seething white came another, twenty or thirty feet back, and then another, until three softly gurgling, splashing waves washed across into the lagoon. Donald and Faaone stood knee-deep in the curded foam, waiting until it had passed so that they could see the coral again.

Donald felt that he could never tire of this, even if he were alone. Out here, far offshore, with the pearl-crowned peaks high above, the long winding reef curving away out of sight, the boom and crash of surf, the rippling song of the water, the flash of colored fish, the sweet salt scent of the sea, he would be content.

But there was Faaone, and when he watched her he was blind to all else. *The Reef Girl!* She was fishing with the long spear. She chased fish into holes and brought them out impaled on the iron. Throwing the spear, however, did not bring her results, to her great annoyance. To Donald she was a magnificent and savage picture of grace in her scant red pareu. With the long spear poised level and quivering, she would stalk a fish, stealthily step by step, and suddenly throw it swift as an arrow. After

156

a number of unsuccessful attempts she swore heartily, to Donald's amusement.

"Don, I am what you call lousy," she said. "Out of practice. I could do better swimming after them. You try."

Donald soon learned that, if their meat depended upon his prowess with a spear, they would starve. But aside from the fun of it, he felt a strong urge to master that age-old method of hunting fish. He would ask Punerie to teach him. They turned back toward the canoe and the opening in the reef, where the rollers came in.

"The tide has turned," said Faaone, her bright eyes upon the sea. "Let us watch the waves a little. Then I shall make you pleased with Faaone."

They sat side by side on a slab of coral that had been thrown up on the reef by a storm. The foam ran seething in to bathe their feet. Directly off the end of the reef the coral sloped out, gray green and streaked with purple, a long shelving into deep water. Its peculiar formation accounted for the extraordinary rising and falling of the swells. The width of the Pacific was behind every wave.

From the shore Donald had often watched the surf at this point, always a contending, shifting tide of blue and green and white. But, impressive as that had been, it was nothing compared to the spectacle he now beheld.

Evidently he and Faaone had arrived just at the end of a series of waves.

"There will not be any for a while," explained Faaone. "But, by-and-by, they will come. You will not believe your eyes. Tahiti has only one grander set of waves, and they are off Vairao."

The sea appeared calm, with only a slight heave in its glassy surface. Fish shapes flashed in the sunlight. Then far out, perhaps half a mile, a dark line rose magically upon the sea. It moved reef-ward, the birth of a swell. White terns fluttered above it, darting down to the water. It lengthened on that side

157

parallel with the reef. Slowly it moved in, gradually it swelled. Beyond it another shadowy line appeared, and farther out another, and still farther another.

The first swell gathered momentum. An invisible and mighty force had seized upon it, quickening, augmenting, endowing it with life. Five hundred yards out it took shape and color. It mounted and curled and broke into billowing white. The second wave, larger, faster, rose and rolled on the heels of the first. The third stretched its curved green front a mile down the reef and fell over with a booming roar. The white tumult of foam came rushing at Donald and Faaone, forcing them to stand erect upon the block of coral.

"There! This one!" screamed Faaone in Donald's ear.

A wall of green sea loomed over the hollow left by the preceding swells. It moved in ponderously, a mountain of water with a long shining summit. Its tremendous volume carried it closer in, past the place where the smaller waves had broken. Suddenly it was awe-inspiring and grand, a green slope curving toward the sky, with a level rim as far down the reef as Donald could see. A shadow darkened the green. It was the rising crest, obscuring the sunlight. All along the magnificent face of the swell the crest leaped high, to curl with the sunlight shining through, to fall forward over a mile-long tunnel, and to plunge down that steep green slope with an appalling thundering roar. A chaos of white and rainbow tints seethed toward the reef.

Faaone had her arms aloft, and she was screaming with rapture. Donald added his cry to hers, mere whispers on the wind. They clung to each other, while the white curded foam rose to their hips. Swell after swell, lessening in power and grandeur as swiftly as they had arisen, followed until again the sea was calm.

"Don, don't you love them? Could you leave them?" cried Faaone, taking his hand. "Come."

She led him up the reef beyond the shelf of conflicting tides. Deep blue water, like that in the lagoon, cut into the reef to an apex. Here the surge rose and fell away abruptly. Across the width of this cove, some two hundred feet out, a ledge of coral showed yellow, and upon this barrier a lazy secondary swell broke to spread its white foam and lose its force in the deep water.

Donald was at once struck by the singular beauty and lack of violence in this particular nook. Beyond the shelf of coral a swell arose, thin and as green as emerald, through which the sunlight shone, and gold, black-barred and green and purple fish sported, like animated jewels. They rose with the swell, and as it came on over the shelf disappeared in the foam.

Fascinated, Donald mounted a black coral head that stood up a couple of feet from the reef. As he did so something red struck him lightly in the face, obscuring his sight. At the same instant he heard Faaone's cry, somehow sweeter and wilder, more piercing than ever before. He tore off the thing—it was Faaone's pareu—just in time to see her dive like an arrow off the ledge.

She went under, down into the clear blue, imbued with marvelous grace and life. The surge rose up and up, to come roaring over the reef. And Faaone came up with it, flashing gold in the sun, to toss her black head and give Donald a dazzling smile.

"Come, Don! Come!" she cried.

"Not on your life!" he yelled. "Have a heart, Faaone! You scared me silly. How in hell will you ever get up out of there? What about the baby?"

But she was either deaf or oblivious to his appeal. She glided about with marvelous ease and exquisite grace, now on the surface with quick powerful strokes, again under, to shoot deep, a long slender golden shape, her black hair streaming out, to come up and roll and roll, and float with her face under, her hands waving gently. Then she swirled on the surface, to swim with swift overhand strokes toward the submerged reef. She went around it and beyond.

The slow emerald swell rose with her and carried her up and

forward. As it curled its tip into a snowy crest, she was gone into its body like a flash of gold, like the colored fish that disported there with her.

Donald stood spellbound. The great swell fell to ruin and rolled its wreaths of white foam over the yellow reef. Beyond in the green water Faaone's black head bobbed up, and she waved a golden arm to Donald. He waved back, stifling his fear. Faaone was at home there. She was a mermaid. Donald thought of the Lorelei of the enchanted rocks, calling sailors to their doom. The artist and poet in him claimed this time, this place, this girl, as the full sum of beauty. The mellow resounding roar, the blazing sun and blue sky, the loneliness of this strip of coral, and Faaone, out there, flashing, weaving, floating like a golden, black-threaded flower on the waves—who other among white men had ever seen the like? Faaone was the Reef Girl. She was coral and sea and fish and the gold of the sun. The life in the exotic flower of the tropics beat in her.

Finally, as he watched, transported, asking no more, she rode the great swell on its crest, her arms flung aloft, her hair flying black against the spindrift, to come floating on the curded foam across the coral shelf. Nearing the ledge she hung feet down in the azure water, her hair floating like black seaweed in the current, while her slim hands kept her afloat. She watched the surge rise against the ledge. It fell back and sank with gurgling roar, to rise again. Faaone kept out of the backwash. Then came the big swell. She propelled herself with it, to rise and rise on its swelling bosom, to flash feet first over the ledge on a bed of snowy foam. She rose before Donald like the goddess of love born of the sea.

"Don, could your—blonde sweetheart—have done that?" panted Faaone, in proud mockery.

Her voice and the content of her words broke the spell that had held Donald enthralled. For one breathless moment he succumbed to the heaving glistening loveliness of her, the black

160

and gold glory of her nudity. Then, reluctantly, he folded the pareu around her.

"Faaone! Girl of two natures, I know now why your people call you the Reef Girl."

"Why do they call me that?" she asked, surprised by his earnestness.

"Because all they see and feel and hear on this coral reef, all the mystery for them of this vast ocean and the island that gave you birth, the sun-god that blazes down upon them, are embodied in your physical perfection, in your passion, in the intense life and spirit of you."

"Donald!" She said no more, but in silence took his hand and walked with him to the canoe. They stepped in, and Faaone took up the paddle to shove off. As they headed home, the seething foam slipped all around them, and the driven fish scurried off the shoal.

13

*

*

*

It seemed to Donald that after his marvelous day with Faaone on the reef he was closer to all elemental things. He and Faaone had nothing to do but play on the reef, roam up the river, gather food and prepare their simple meals, and sleep in each other's arms. With Faaone, he grasped happiness for the first time in his life. But as he felt the baby growing within her, he felt a mounting sense of uncertainty. As strong as he had become, his upbringing rose to confront him—his child must not be a nameless bastard, as were so many of the children on this island.

With his realization of this, some of the old memories revived. He had forgotten about his mail and his contacts with home. Somehow, now that he was to have a child, they had achieved a new significance.

One day he announced, "Faaone, we must go to Papeete again. We're running low on supplies, and we can't get them from Hing's. And I must look at my mail."

Her face clouded. "Donald, must we? We have been so happy here. I am afraid of the mail from overseas. It will take you away from me!"

"Nonsense, darling. Besides you must see the doctor—just as

a precaution. And we both need new clothes."

Finally she consented to go, but Donald could see that she was unhappy about it.

"Darling, I want to buy you a striking new outfit from Paris —you'll stun all the gossipers at the Cercle Bougainville."

"Donald, do you really want to be seen with me openly—your Tahitian mistress?"

"My Tahitian wife," he said emphatically. "As far as anyone who cares is concerned, you are my wife."

They were up at dawn, had their breakfast before Tiare arrived, and were down at Hing's before the Tautira bus. When it came, Donald and Faaone climbed into the first seat behind the driver. The villagers, for whom the arrival and departure of the bus was always an event, loaded on fruit, chickens, pigs, and voiced merry farewells to passengers going to town.

This time Donald took keen interest in the scenery presented on the journey to Papeete. The road climbed around the most rugged part of the island past Hitiaa, in one place going high above the sounding sea, and in several others rounding rocky points where a rough surf beat upon stone parapets. Looking down, he could see the green coral and the short swells pounding on the rocks. For several miles there was no barrier reef outside, only a faint green line of submerged coral. Swift clear streams poured down out of the mountains, and long stretches of the road were lined with hibiscus trees and colored leaf hedges, behind which glimpses of pretty native cottages could be seen. This north side of Tahiti appeared to Donald to be the most picturesque shoreline, and the least inhabited. Two little islets, green and white, some distance offshore, particularly took his eye; then a long strip, where the combers rolled in upon a boulder-strewn beach. The road ran for what seemed hours along shores of black rock, deeply cut and indented by the tides, where the waves curled in to buffet and crash, sending high the flying spray. Here, at one stop, Faaone showed him the rarest fish around Tahiti, little jumping creatures a few inches long, black as coal, that lived half-in and half-out of the water. Donald saw them flit from one bare rock to another as the surf splashed over.

Eventually the bus turned inland to climb a steep ascent around a great promontory. It came out on top, close to the rim a thousand feet above the sea, where one of the supremely magnificent views of Tahiti emerged. This, Faaone told Donald, was the place to which the tourists and sightseers were taken to look at the leagues of barrier reef, at Venus Point, and, beyond across the blue channel, at Moorea half-lost in pearl clouds.

Up here the road was rough and full of chuckholes, a tribute to the incessant storms that were blown by the trade winds into the mountains on the north shore. But this morning it was clear and bright, with only a handful of white clouds obscuring the dark green peaks of the mountains.

The road wound around this plateau for several hours, stopping to load or unload passengers at the tiny villages on the route. But Donald was so engrossed by the magnificence of the scenery that he failed to notice the passage of time, until the bus bumped around the headlands of Venus Point, and he saw the red and green smokestacks of the monthly steamer at the dock. It was ship-day and most of Papeete would be on hand to greet it.

"I shall meet you later, Don. You will want to read your mail," Faaone said, a little haltingly.

He squeezed her arm. "Thanks, Faaone. I'll see you at Cercle Bougainville at three."

She turned away with such a wistful smile that he said, "Come on, darling, keep your promise and be happy. I will meet you later. I do want people to see you with me."

Donald went down the wide familiar street, walking, like the other pedestrians, in the streets. Cars went honking by, some with tourists, some with white uniformed officials, others with lei-decorated native girls, sensuous and bold-eyed.

164

Papeete, as always, was hot and oppressive. No breeze came to cool the air, which smelled of copra mixed with dust. For several blocks Donald did not recognize either white man or native. None of those who passed him gave him a second glance. Remembering his good friend the barber, he entered the shop on the corner opposite the quay. There, while waiting his turn, he resisted a yearning to pick up an American magazine or look at the wireless ship newspaper. Presently he was in the chair, sitting with closed eyes and letting the barber do his work. Georges talked as rapidly as he worked the scissors. But like all Frenchmen he was discreet and courteous. The only way he reminded Donald of the past was to compliment him upon his fine appearance—brown as a native, and looking fit. He was full of news. Papeete was losing its resident Americans and tourist traffic due to the devaluation of the American dollar. Business was very poor. The new tariff law of the United States had turned all the copra trade into French channels, and copra was selling at sixty centimes a kilogram; the Tahitians were hard-hit and would have to return to their fish and fruit diet. A young American couple had been stranded in Tahiti and were operating a little restaurant. Donald should patronize them.

"Are the Bellairs still here?" asked Donald.

"Yes. I shaved Monsieur Bellair this morning. He will be delighted to see you. He always asks about you. Of course, no one knows anything about you."

"How about the coconut radio?"

"Ah monsieur, that is different. If you want native gossip . . ."

"No thanks, Georges. But I should think everybody would know about me."

"They say times were bad for you for a while. Then they improved again. I have only to see you, Monsieur Perth, to know that is true. Believe me, I am happy."

Donald left in lighter spirit and walked across the street toward MacGregor's. A row of native women sat on the stone

165

pavement offering leis and hula skirts for sale. He was recognized, for one dark-eyed girl offered him a lei with a knowing smile that meant: "Frangipani for Faaone!" Donald gave her a few francs and took the fragrant lei. Attentive gazes were visited upon him as he passed the curio stores and bars on the way to the post office. Unfortunately, it was still closed for the noonday interval, as the crowd of all races that was waiting there proved.

Crossing the road to the quay, Donald found a shaded seat on one of the stone benches. The scene was as interesting as if this had been his first sight of the copper-hued lagoon, glistening under a fiery sun. All was as before—the green quarantine island and the great white rollers on the reef, the copra schooners moored to the trees, bursting with their cargo, the idlers, the bicyclers, the stream of autos passing by. The same Tahitian girls, it seemed, were patrolling the street, brown-skinned, generously built, with long dark braids down their straight backs, walking like princesses—the streetwalkers of Tahiti.

Suddenly the shrill honk of a horn distracted Donald; a shiny green car halted opposite him. The driver was Bellair. He leaned out the open window to shout, while Donald rose to meet him.

"Hello Perth," Bellair said heartily, wringing Donald's hand. "I heard you were in town again. God, I'm glad to see you!"

"Thanks—it's good to see you, too, Bell," returned Donald.

"You look great! Better than I ever saw you. On the level! You're thin, but hard. Been fishing, eh? And swimming with Faaone—we just met her up the street. Catherine is with her now. My God, Perth, how lovely she looks! She saved you, and you saved her—that's what the coconut radio says. I'll be damned if it isn't true!"

"Well, it's a fact Faaone saved me."

"I never would have believed it. I don't trust the coconut radio. Or Tahiti. Still you may prove the exception. . . . The radio says you're going to marry her. Are you?"

166

"No. She won't have me. At least not yet."

"Faint heart, you know . . . But more power to you. I'll say this. What we Americans call the world is well lost for that girl. If only you can hold on to her!"

"Perhaps I don't deserve her."

"Nonsense! It's the other way around. . . . Are you writing again?"

"Writing? Oh-h, no, I've quite forgotten all that," Donald said lamely.

"Better go back to it. We whites must have something to keep us busy. If it weren't for my fishing I'd drink myself to death."

"I thought you were on the wagon?"

"No, I'm not. Fell off for the last time. It's simply unendurable, insupportable, impossible, not to drink in the tropics. But I don't guzzle it like I used to."

"That's good to hear," responded Donald. He noted, however, that Bellair's hands, as he lighted a fresh cigarette, shook a little more than formerly. The shadow, too, on the New Englander's face, now that the warmth and smile had faded, was more marked than ever.

"Bell—I want to thank you for being so decent the last time I was here. I realize now, of course, you must have known about me and Faaone."

"Sure, old chap. But you were so distraught. I didn't want to ask about her. But it's all for the best now."

"Has Catherine heard from Winifred?" asked Donald, trying to be casual.

"Several times. There was a letter on Saturday's boat."

"How— Is she well?"

"Not very, as a matter of fact. She's never recovered from some kind of poisonous infection in her leg, something she contracted here. She's had a hell of a time, had to walk with a crutch for a long while. Haven't *you* heard from her?"

"I've not asked for my mail since . . ." He did not finish the sentence. Then he added, "But I shall today."

167

"You do that little thing, Don. Winifred has been crazy to hear something about you. All Catherine could tell her was what the natives told us, and not much of that could we pass on. You will write her, won't you? She still loves . . ."

"Have a heart, Bell," choked out Donald, averting his face a moment until the sudden storm in his breast had quieted. Finally he went on. "Tell me something about Bennet-Stokes. Georges didn't mention him, come to think of it."

"That blighter!" exclaimed Bellair. "Haven't you heard about him?"

"Nothing, except what you told me that day—that he was in the hospital. Faaone did tell me that he's not her father—that he no longer has a claim on her."

"No, he isn't her father. We all know that now. But didn't Faaone tell you what happened to him?"

"No, she didn't," Donald said, his pulse pounding. "Bennet-Stokes has not been mentioned since— She has forgotten him."

"But she must know! My God, the news flashed over the coconut radio here as if Marconi was at the mike. Faaone couldn't help but hear what all the natives knew long ago. She's kept it from you."

"What did happen?" returned Donald, his emotions in tight check.

"Bennet-Stokes has been gone for weeks."

"Gone? Left Tahiti?"

"Right. And a damn good riddance. He left on a French freighter, bound for Le Havre."

"On a freighter? How come?"

"He didn't dare risk a regular steamer," rejoined Bellair, as he nervously threw away his half-finished cigarette to light another.

"What the hell? Come clean, Bell, will you?"

"Bennet-Stokes had leprosy. He was afraid that if he took a passenger ship he would be stopped at Le Havre. And it's a cinch he would have been if the French officials here had been

168

wise to what he had. But they haven't found out yet. Or if they have, they've kept silent."

"What did you say was—wrong with Stokes?"

"He had leprosy, poor devil! Malignant leprosy . . ." Bellair stopped, suddenly aware of the effect his words were having. For a long time neither man spoke. Then Bellair said, "Shall we have a drink, Don?"

Donald started. "No, no. I'm sorry— I promised Faaone . . ."

"Right—I'll be seeing you."

Though he had always suspected what had happened, Donald had never asked Faaone about it. He had assumed she was present when Moto died, and he had known the hypodermic was missing from his body. He had not wanted to know more. But now his reaction surprised him. There was a sense of shock and even horror at Bennet-Stokes's tragedy, at the form Faaone's revenge had taken. But she had once told him that a native only killed a white by cunning. And it was for him she had done this thing, protecting him the only way she could! Who was he to condemn her, he who had killed for far less reason? And the method, after all, was the one Bennet-Stokes had planned to use on him.

Now that he knew what he had only suspected, he felt more than anything else a sense of relief, and a love, a tenderness, for Faaone greater than before. During all the joy and happiness they had shared after she had returned with him, she had harbored her terrible secret and pretended for his sake that it did not exist. This must be why she had refused to marry him. Now that he knew, somehow he must dispel her haunting fears and bring her back to the joys they had shared. He loved her, and he meant to marry her.

A bustle in front of the post office finally caught his attention. The doors had been opened. The colorful crowd jostled on the high stone steps and in the doorway.

He wondered for a moment if it might be better never to

open a letter from the home and country he had abandoned. But the trustee of the little money that had been left him would have sent remittances. He needed money. He ought not to live wholly upon Faaone. He got up, strode across the street, and took his place in the line with the Tahitians and whites of several nationalities. He recognized the faces of several people, but no one there appeared ever to have seen him before. Presently his turn came at the window where, in his poor French, he asked for his mail.

He was amazed at the bundle of papers and letters that was handed out to him. He carried it out, aware of a little dimness in his eyes, and that he jostled passers-by. What should he do with all this mail—all this printed matter, which had to do with a past irrevocably gone? The parcel had been securely tied, and a packet of the latest letters slipped under the string. Donald looked at the top one curiously. The handwriting blurred in his sight. Then he caught a faint fragrance, and it tore his heart with an incredible pang. Winifred's Pois de Santeur! Donald's half-made decision not to read his mail—to open only envelopes from his bank—went into eclipse. He still had an identity that had not been lost to the Tahitian reefs! He was still Donald Perth. And it was manifest that he had not been forgotten.

Returning to the bench he untied the parcel, then the packet, and separated the letters. So many of the large white envelopes with their seductive perfume! His hands shook as he consigned these to his pocket. There were three envelopes carrying the name and address of his bank. These he opened to extract the drafts, which represented three quarterly payments of his small income. The sum seemed a fortune to him now. Tying up the bundle again he hurried up the street to MacGregor's, where he was sure the cashier would identify him and honor the drafts. Not only was he identified by this official, but very pleasantly surprised by a remark in English.

"I saw you fishing the Tautira last Sunday. Great run of nato!"

"Ah! Indeed it was. Are you a nato fisherman?" asked Donald.

"Yes, indeed. But not as good as Faaone," he replied, with a smile.

When their transactions were completed, Donald found himself the possessor of twelve thousand francs. Suddenly he had a wild desire to spend them! His first purchase, however, was a grass basket in which he deposited his mail and the rolls of bills in small denominations. The five-hundred-franc notes he stowed away in his pocket. Then he sauntered out upon the street. The fragrance of Winifred's letters inspired him to go first into Tung Hing's and ask Ah You for Pois de Santeur. Ah You remembered him well.

"Faaone was in," he said. "More beautiful than ever! But not the old Faaone. You are the one lucky man in her life!"

"Yes? That is good. What did she buy?"

"Nothing yet. Faaone is no longer extravagant. She liked the flowered Chinese silk, but said that she would come back."

"I'll buy it, Ah You. And when she comes back, give it to her. But—don't tell her about the Pois de Santeur. . . . Oh, yes, I want safranor, too."

From there Donald went on up the street to Madame Reamy's, where, from that delighted French tradeswoman, he learned that Faaone had been in to try on the gorgeous pink hat from Paris. The price was one hundred and sixty-five francs. Donald bought it and left it to be delivered to Faaone upon her return. Then he thought of the new American restaurant and made his way there to lunch. The young owners were exceedingly pleasant, but the curiosity of other customers reminded Donald that he was one of Tahiti's famous—or notorious—characters. He heard the whispered words "gone native" and "beachcomber" and regretted the eagerness that had led him here. But he stuck it out, even to being civil to a tourist who accosted him. After his lunch, he retired to a shady seat on the quay and slowly, with bated breath and against his resolve to wait, broke the wax seal of Winifred's letter of latest date. He read:

Don darling:

Why don't you answer my letters? You must not have received them. I have written letters on end, and the longer this silence of yours persists the more fearful I get.

Surely you would have written about mother's death. In her way she was fond of you. We had scarcely been home a month, as I wrote you, when she died suddenly of a heart attack.

The estate has been settled. Don, she left you a hundred thousand, provided you married me. And I find myself worth a million. I'm a rich girl, Don! Why don't you come back and take me, beat me, marry me? You see? All that pride and imperiousness you were wont to criticize is gone forever.

But before this epistle degenerates into raving importunity, let me tell you the good news about my leg. It was terrible, as you must know, for weeks and weeks after I returned home. The doctors gave my malady a lot of names, scientific and otherwise, but the fact is they were puzzled. They didn't know what it was. The turn for the better came lately. Almost too good to be true! The pain has almost all gone, and the swelling has subsided, until I can recognize my once-beautiful foot. Don, you always said I had the shapeliest feet and legs you ever saw on a girl. You used to say, too, that I like to show them off too much. Well, thank heaven, my bad one is now on the mend. I can walk again, and soon I'll be able to dance. Dance! Don, do you get that? But I must have my slim, elegant partner back, otherwise I can never dance again or live again.

Oh, Donald, it was in your ghastly and glorious Tahiti that I really learned to love you. Love you! I have been a vain, selfish, heedless thing, a cat, a flirt—it took something appalling to bring me to my senses.

I almost died when you disappeared. When they found the car they thought you had committed suicide. Catherine Bellair's letters drive me mad. She's friendly and fine, and it's

172

obvious that she's miserable when she writes me, because she has so little news of you.

But she knows you are alive and well, after some awful experience or other. You are living with Faaone, she writes. Darling, I have not one little word of scorn or reproach or hate to utter. But jealous? I am consumed with it. I remember that girl's incomparable beauty.

Only Don, despite Faaone, you can't stay there forever. You can't give up your work forever. How I blame myself for ridiculing your ambition to write! I wanted you to be my cavalier, my attendant, my lover, husband, and slave. But I was wrong. You have a gift. I had no sense and not enough intellect to realize it.

Don, surely you know that your book will be published this fall. A representative of your publishing house has been here to call on me. He wanted news of you, personal and intimate things to print for publicity, photographs, and what not. I gave him all I could. And assured him that you were alive and well—that you would come home soon.

Just think, Don. He said you had genius. Genius! My God, how that word hurt me! All the time you were a genius!

Don, darling, I can be big. I will. If I have lost you—well, I'll endure it if only you will come home. If I killed your love for me, don't let that ruin you, keep you from your career.

And that brings me to a betrayal of myself.

Donald, I am obsessed by a desire to return to Tahiti. Never, never could I go, but the longing sometimes is almost unbearable.

What happened to me there, Donald? By now you must know the truth about that island's monstrous and ineffable charm. I can see the green slopes rising to the purple peaks and the pearl clouds, the dark canyons with their white-fringed waterfalls, the blaze of flowers, the blue lagoon, and the reef. I can hear the wind blow down from the heights, the rustle of *the palms, the roar of rain on the roof, the morning song of the mynah birds, the thunder of the surf. And I can smell the unforgettable fragrance of Tahiti. The scent of frangipani blossoms comes back to me with a sweetness that is devastation.*

I can feel the hot sun on my back and arms and legs. Oh, it feels so good! But Don, when the moon shines full, I crawl into my bed in the dark and cover my head and fight a maddening mockery. Sun and moon of Tahiti—they were my undoing!

Write, Don, please write, anything to ease my conscience and my fear.

Winifred

Such was the letter in Donald's hand. But he stared at it unseeing after reading the middle paragraphs. "Well, I'll be damned! Has Win gone crazy? Book? Publisher? *Genius?*"

He fumbled among the other letters to find the long official-looking envelope that had in the left-hand corner a familiar letterhead. With numb hands he tore it open. Out fell a folded blue paper and a typewritten letter, at the top of which was secured a check. His manuscript!— Acceptance!— Praise!— Contract!— Check! Letter and contents fell from Donald's nervous hands. While he scraped them up, thoughts like a terrible army arrayed with banners and spikes rushed at him, as if from the outside, from the crackling paper in his fist. Yes, there was the sea before him, the island at his back, real as the torrid sun that beat down. But now, out of that blue north had come this thunderbolt. The girl he had loved so dearly, the career he had yearned for—his, his for the taking, but oh, the burning hell of it! It came too late—too late!

14

❋

❋

❋

Faaone finally located Donald at the bar in Kelly's.

"So there you are. When you did not show up at Cercle Bougainville, I started looking." Her strong little hand grabbed his arm. The noisy hall, the roistering groups around the pool tables, the pall of yellow smoke, the white-clad sailors at the tables with native girls, all whirled about him. In the center of the cyclone Faaone stood, her great eyes troubled.

"What's wrong?" asked Donald, bracing himself.

Faaone did not reply, but her expression of regret changed to strong concern. Punerie stood beside her, loaded with bundles. He grinned knowingly, and removing the handle of Donald's basket from around his neck, he slipped an arm under his. Faaone took the other arm, and together they led him out of the bar.

"I'm all right—Faa. . . . not drunk at all," he said.

"No, darling. What happened to you?"

"Damn if I know," mumbled Donald. The sudden emergence into the sunlight and the cool late afternoon breeze made him dizzy. They helped him to the bus, boosted him into it, and the last that Donald remembered was his head in Faaone's lap.

He awoke from his stupefying slumber sometime the following morning. He lay on the bed, dressed as he had been in Papeete, except for the canvas shoes. His head ached, but his mind was clear. Faaone sat by the table, on which he saw his letters and papers and the beautiful pink hat he had purchased at Madame Reamy's. Her face bore a look of profound sorrow, and her great eyes were dark with pain.

"I don't know what came over me, Faa—the old pain, the old fears. I guess I just couldn't take it sober."

"I know. I read her letter," whispered Faaone tragically.

"Darling, that wasn't the reason," said Donald. "I swear it wasn't!"

"She will come after you and take you away from me."

"No! Didn't you read she said she could never come back to Tahiti?"

"Then you will go home to her. That golden-haired vampire! She is rich now."

"Faaone, listen. I won't leave you."

"You lie, white man! You are false, like all your race. . . . You love her still!" Faaone spent her strength in those words, and suddenly, blinded by tears, she staggered to the bed to fall into his arms.

"Faa, don't break down," he pleaded, holding her close. "Maybe I do still love Winifred—a little, anyway. Maybe I'm one of those people who never gets over love. But, my princess of Tahiti—you are my life's blood, my soul itself. I could not live without you."

"But, lover, you got drunk—just because she—"

"No! I drank because I was crazy. Faaone, you read the letter. It was because of my book. It was accepted. Didn't you see the check? Money sent to me in advance!"

He succeeded eventually in averting the storm of her fear and grief, but it was his embrace, his devouring kisses, more than his protestations, that did it. Finally her sobs subsided, and

176

she said, "Book? I didn't read that far. . . . I—didn't see any check."

"Here, it's in this letter. Look!"

"Darling, I—I can't see. Read it to me."

Donald did so, with a break in his husky voice. The news, the truth leaped at him, to stagger him again. Faaone sat up and looked at him with dilated and still-dewy eyes. She was quick enough to grasp the sense of fortune in that letter, if not its deep significance to Donald.

"Five thousand dollars! For a book?— Don, how wonderful!"

"That's only an advance. If the book is as good as Win—as evidently the publisher believes—it will earn a lot more!"

"You will be a great writer!" she cried, her eyes shining now. "Like Stevenson and Melville!"

"Hardly, Faaone," murmured Donald, lowering his eyes. He thought, I must get away—alone! This was intolerable!

"But, Don, you will not stop. You will go on. You must tell my story—*our* story! Oh, I have kept so much from you!"

"Our story would be great, Faaone. But I will never write again."

"Of course you will," she said. Her rich vibrant voice pierced Donald's consciousness, leaving his heart heavy.

"Faaone! I might—if—if you would go back to America with me, so I could find out if this good news is really true. And find my worth, Faaone, in the eyes of my own people."

"America!" She whispered. "Oh, Don, do not ask me to leave Tahiti."

"Only for a while, darling," he implored. "Only a few months."

"I could not. I would wither away if I were taken from Tahiti— You would not see your golden vahine again! Aue! No —no!" And becoming incoherent she ran out of the house. Donald thought it best to leave her alone. Tiare called him to breakfast, which he ate by himself. After that he went back into the living room and, searching in his basket, found his money intact. The five-hundred-franc notes were still folded in his pocket. The two letters were there, too, Winifred's on the table, the publisher's on the bed. Evidently Faaone had looked over the other letters, but she had not opened any sealed ones. Donald had an idea he would not open any more either, at least not for a while. He put the letters and money in the bottom of Faaone's chest, and striding out of the house, he took the trail up the valley and was soon lost in the jungle.

He realized the thing which stung him most cruelly was not the fact that he could not leave Faaone to go home to New England but the vividness and poignancy of his stirred memory. He had imagined, even if he had not wholly forgotten Winifred and his ambition, that he had ceased to care. But Winifred's incredible letter, with its confessions and yearnings, its proof of a sleepless remorse, had uncovered the old wound. It bled afresh and burned and throbbed with love and hope that had really never died. He was Donald Perth again, the younger man, gazing at himself with these older eyes, at what might have been.

He wandered beyond the trail into the wilderness, like a deer stricken to death that must crawl into the remotest place, there to lie down with only the eye of nature upon him. He found a place he had never seen, a deep spring, source of one of the streams that gushed from a rock-strewn, fern-decked glade, open to the hot sun and surrounded by huge purau trees, whose yellow flowers scented the drowsy air. It was a spot where he would have liked to die. Dulled as was his sense of beauty, he still saw and felt the irresistible force of Tahiti's eternal summer, of the green, gold, pearl, blue loveliness that mocked while it fettered.

"Why did I read those letters?" he cried, voicing aloud the bitter question in his mind. "I *knew* no good would come of it. This is insufferable. Am *I* two persons, like Faaone?— How much easier for me if Win had written of well-being, of marriage, of just kind remembrance of me! But *this*—that she at last loves me as I always wanted, but was sure she couldn't— And that my secret belief, my secret dream, has come true—true! How can I bear to know that and not be there!"

It did not help much to plunge down into a mossy niche among the stones and hide his face from the blaze of the sun and the amber light of the walls of yellow flowers. He could shut out his environment, this lonely tropic prison that must be his to the end of his hateful days, but in the eyes of his mind he saw it—and saw, in contrast, Winifred and the praise of his fellows and all that achievement meant in America.

If only he had not known! Faaone was beauty and love incarnate. That had sufficed for him. But now, would they ever be the same again? He could not leave her. There was nothing as black-hearted as ingratitude. Besides, stronger even than the clutch of this South Sea paradise, than all that there was left of love and honor in his heart, was the terrible physical hold this half-native woman had on him. It was unbreakable. He never wanted to break it!

A long drowsy sigh out of the jungle washed over him. It was the breath of the sea and the island, fragrant, intoxicating— boundlessly unlike the stir and the unrest, the stimulus of civilization. Plumed bamboo stalks dropped out of the flowered wall of green—rustling, whispering, shivering in the gentle zephyr. Donald paced to and fro, trampling a trail in the ferns. If nature was God and God breathed everywhere in this wilderness, some strength, some peace, should come to him. But the vigil of the day wore on without either.

In the waning afternoon, he retraced his steps. Faaone ran off the porch to meet him, and her kisses, her embraces, her broken words, were indicative of the great fear that had arisen during his absence. She had little to say. She hung around him, seemingly unmindful of his coldness, and waited upon him at supper like a slave.

When darkness came, and Donald discarded his wet clothes

for a pareu and lay down upon the bed, then Faaone glided stealthily to him, naked, fragrant as the frangipani blossoms in her hair. Donald felt suddenly that he had to fight the native in her, the savage passion that had bound him to her so irrevocably. Gentle and responsive as he had always been, even grateful for the lavishing of her pagan charms, now he repulsed her. That only inflamed her ardor.

"Faaone, have a heart!" he implored, wearily. "I understand. I know how you feel. And I—I'll never leave you. I swear to God I won't. . . ."

But Faaone gave no heed, if she even heard his importuning. She imagined that she might lose her white man and that there was only one way to keep him.

For Donald, since the beginning of their love together, there had been no hope of resisting her love-making, even if he had desired to. But tonight, when he felt swelling in him that warm and languorous wave, that drifting away to exquisite sensibilities, he thought of the sacrifice he was making for her. He grew angry, and he struck her, knocking her off the bed. The blow, scarcely a brutal one, somehow liberated the fury that once before had possessed him utterly. He sprang from the bed, his eyes searching for something to beat her with. Moonlight filtered in through the chinks between the bamboos, silvering the room, reminding him mercilessly of that other night. Seizing one of the slender cane poles in the corner, he broke off the tip and turned upon Faaone.

She was on her knees, her hand to her cheek, her naked form clear in the moonlight.

"Damn—you," cried Donald. "You beautiful—cat! . . ."

He struck her sharply over the shoulders. Faaone uttered a cry, low like that of a surprised and hurt child, and fell face down upon the floor. He struck her naked back again, and again. After the third blow, the slip of bamboo broke in his hands. She made no sound, no movement.

Then his frenzy faded, and he flung himself upon the bed, his

180

mind awakening to the horror of what he had done. He wanted to lift Faaone up. Still, he did not, and presently she arose from the floor. Quietly she lay down beside him and crept weeping into his arms. Donald felt her hot tears on his chest. Her perfumed hair rippled down to cover him, and her warm breasts pressed against his side. He reached down to pull the coverlet over them.

But Donald could not sleep. Long after Faaone had ceased to cry and had fallen asleep in his arms, her dark head on his shoulder, he lay awake, filled with terrible remorse. He had beaten Faaone, whom he loved above all else. There was a full moon, and a flood tide was thundering on the reef. The night, barring the sea, was as still as death. There in the quiet room, Donald saw himself trapped by that beautiful flower-like face upon his breast, doomed to the haunting call of the reef and the slow atrophy of memory and loss of identity and fame.

At sunrise he went out, hoping to prevent the return of his phantoms in the morning light. An exquisitely soft glow mantled the slope. Ashen clouds obscured the distant mountains, but from behind the eastern hills rolled glorious columns of gold and rose. Below them mists of pale pearl shone silver against the green. And all these lovely forms and colors were reflected in the lagoon. But even as he stood praying for the old enchantment, there came a change that killed his hope. All was changed. There was nothing that lasted.

Upon going into the house again, he found Faaone awake. Her big eyes lighted up at sight of him.

"Don, I was afraid," she said, a slow smile coming.

"Of what? Tupapa'us?"

"No. You were gone. . . ."

Silence lay between them, like a barrier reef. He wanted to tell her that he loved her, ask her forgiveness, but the words would not come. Finally, almost harshly, he said, "Get up, Faaone. We must eat. Then I must work—or else I will go crazy."

He saw a question in her thoughtful eyes, but she did not

voice it. Nor did she mention the beating. But as she sat up, stretching, she turned her back to his gaze. The gold loveliness of that perfect form was marred by red stripes, the sight of which hurt Donald more than any words she might have uttered.

After breakfast they went down to the lagoon, accompanied by Tupa, laden with poles and baskets. Donald carried a paddle and spear. Faaone wore her pareu high up.

With the sun an hour high, Tahiti was at its loveliest. The lagoon shone like green emeralds. A flood of rose and golden light spread over mountain, vale, and sea. The mynah birds sang like mocking birds; the little white terns fluttered over the lagoon; native women stood knee-deep in the water on the reef, their long poles extended; far out a group of fishermen were beating the sea with paddles, driving fish into their net. Donald felt something like a new birth of life on the earth. At least here, he thought, there was no horror of war, no complexity of civilization. There really was something grand, something immortal.

All morning they were out on the reef, fishing, wading, swimming, resting in the sunshine. The showers were hot one moment and coolly wet the next. From time to time Donald would pause, hold his pole idle for a moment or lean on his spear, and gaze away across the heaving sea to the north. But these moments occurred less and less often. And when Faaone took to riding the swell, in all her inimitable grace and triumphant love of the sea, then he had no thought of home at all, only the sense of color and action and beauty.

In the afternoon they tramped far up the canyon, were caught in a storm, then dried out in the sun. When their nato basket was full, Donald gave it to Faaone to carry while he gathered fei. Suspending two huge bunches of the red-colored, banana-like fruit from each end of a pole, he balanced it across his shoulders like a native and packed the fruit all the way home. He arrived in the clearing, wet with perspiration, exhausted. That night, scarcely had he felt Faaone slip softly to his side when his eyes closed, and he was lost to thought.

Day after day passed like that, with a variation only in the form of activity. In sun and storm they were out. Little by little Donald's morbid brooding gave way, as it had done before, in communion with the elements and in physical activity. He never read a line of a book or letter. If he thought, now and then, that he was slipping—slipping into the sensorial life of a savage—he did not dwell on it. Faaone and he lived day by day.

But Faaone had changed. She was all sweetness and gentleness and pensiveness. Never since he had beaten her had she come alive with that flaming passion that had fused him into her being. He puzzled over this, conscious of a sense of loss. Could it be that, after all, he did not want her to lose anything of her originality, much less the fire of passionate love, which a few weeks ago had seemed to be destroying him?

One day, after a visit to her mother, she returned at sunset, and he saw her enter the clearing, with that marvelous gold and purple light at her back. He was sitting on the porch steps, aware that he had been waiting for her. What else save Faaone was there for him? Her step was unusually vibrant; her face wore such an ethereal and exquisite glow that he attributed it to the glamour of the sunset, against which it stood out in relief. She approached him slowly and sat down beside him. When he saw her eyes he sat up, transfixed and thrilling, but when he reached for her she twisted out of his arms.

"No!" she said softly, but firmly. "Donald, I want to talk, to tell you something. I have been thinking about this for a long while."

"Darling—"

She put a finger on his lips. "Don, hear me out. You have heard that I have hated all white men. I have hated even you. Even after I loved you, I hated you—in loving you I had lost myself, and I thought that like all white men you would leave your native vahine in the end. But then, after what I did to Bennet-Stokes, you asked me to marry you! I could not say yes,

183

not then. I felt I was not worthy of you. But I held the promise in my heart. And then the post came. When I read that letter from Winifred and saw how it affected you, I was terrified that you would leave me and return to America and your blonde vahine. But you have not left—and now I think you will not go."

"Faaone, you never can lose me, you know that," protested Donald.

Again she touched her finger to his lips. "You will not go, but your heart is not here with me at night. I can feel it slipping away as we lie together."

Suddenly she was crying, great crystal tears following one another down her cheeks. But the rhythm of her speech did not change. "I love you so much I cannot bear to lose your heart, even for a little while. There is nothing in this world for me if you are not part of it. And so, if you still want it—I will come with you to your America. If you still want me, I will marry you."

He gathered her in his arms. His voice was husky. "My darling, there is nothing I want more. I've been so ghastly to you these past weeks I don't even deserve you. But I will always love you and try to be worthy of you."

"Even—even if you see your blonde vahine again?"

"She is a ghost, Faaone. A lovely ghost to be sure, but from a dead past. I swear it."

She clung to him, trembling. With a sudden burst of passion, he stripped her pareu from her and carried her to the bed. He ran his hands over her full breasts, the tender curve of her belly, and her gleaming thighs. Their two bodies locked in an embrace that was more frenzied yet more tender than they had ever known, ending in a great wave of oceanic passion that seemed to engulf them.

When it was over, and they lay together in utter peace, Donald said, "Now, do you have any doubts about our love for each other? Tomorrow we must go to Papeete. You must have the most beautiful gown that Madame Reamy can provide for our

184

wedding day. I'll hire the Tautira stage so all of your people can go in with us to see us married. We'll have a great party—a wedding feast, Faaone."

He stopped to kiss her and went on dreamily. "White people have honeymoons, you know. *We* shall have one. I want to show you everything on our honeymoon, Faaone. We'll start with San Francisco. I want to marry you again there—in my people's church. We'll go to Yosemite, which is almost as beautiful as Tahiti. We'll see the great redwood trees, the orchards and vineyards of California. I'll take you to Hollywood, darling, to see the stars—not one of whom can approach you in beauty. Then we'll fly East—have you ever seen an airplane, darling? —to New York. And there I shall show you . . . Faaone, it's my *home!* It will be yours, too, if you will come. Will you?—"

"Oh, Don!" She nestled against him. "Yes—" She hesitated. Then, firmly: "Yes, I shall come."

In the morning, light-footed and swift, she flew ahead of Donald down the trail to the lower clearing. There she stopped at her mother's house, while he went on to the village. At Hing's he engaged passage for Faaone's wedding party on the stage, and ascertained that the southbound steamer would arrive the next day, Saturday. That meant that the northbound ship would reach Papeete on Monday and sail for San Francisco at dawn on Tuesday morning. What luck! Faaone would have no time to come out of her transport, to recall her strange fear of leaving Tahiti. They would be on that ship bound for America! He found himself treading on air, prey to the most insane exultation.

Faaone waited for him at Matureo's. Contact with her people had added to her state of bliss. The coming child, the wedding, the party, her mother's joy—these possessed Faaone's mind entirely. Hand in hand they walked up the flowered trail, with the sunset at their backs.

Donald halted on the porch, strangely impelled to gaze at the amber pool where nato splashed, at the lacy waterfall, and at the purple canyon with its gold-tipped rims. At the prospect of leaving them, a pang assaulted his heart. Nor did it suffice for him to know that he loved this place beyond any other, that he would return to it. He felt an inexplicable reluctance at the idea of even a brief separation. He only hoped such thoughts would not disturb Faaone's consciousness.

Donald's belongings, such as he wanted to take, were not many and required but little time to pack. Then, while Faaone discarded some things and chose others and changed her mind and talked on distractedly, he paced the porch outside, trying to come down to earth.

The familiar sounds of reef and river, the murmuring of the waterfalls and whisper of the palms seemed sweeter than he had ever heard them. He listened intently, wanting to carry them with him across the sea. Suddenly when his heart seemed full and his ears attuned forever to this melody of Tahiti, a weird and awful cry came down the canyon. It drove away all the haunting sweet voices he had sought to possess. Had he really heard anything? He listened, dreading to make sure, hoping that the cry had been only his ever-treacherous imagination. But just as relief began to flood his consciousness, again the cry came, scarcely discernible, mocking and haunting. And suddenly he thought it might be his own wandering spirit, gone to join the tupapa'us.

"Nonsense!" he muttered. "Am I going native?" Shaken despite his angry repudiation of something beyond a white man's reason, he went in to Faaone. He did not choose to tell her what had happened. While she sorted her treasures, he went to bed, but it was long before he fell into a restless sleep.

In the morning a shower roared down the canyon, eliciting lamentations from Faaone. She complained she would have to go bare-legged down the trail. But the black cloud passed swiftly out to sea and the sun burst out brilliantly, hot and white. Leaves and flowers glistened like diamonds. A fragrant steam rose from the jungle.

186

Faaone walked ahead of Donald down the trail. He, burdened with the baggage and dragged often to a halt by that strange yearning reluctance to leave, made but slow progress. His last long gaze was at the lagoon and the reef, flushed by pink cloud-shadows blazing in patches like burnished mosaics of beaten gold. The hollow roar of the surf seemed to reproach him with his desertion.

All of Fitieu was on hand to see Faaone off to her wedding and her fabulous journey to the distant land of the Americans. Matureo and her other daughters and their friends wore their best garments—all spotless white, contrasting with the dark eager faces, the brown masses of hair, and the red hibiscus blossoms. The bus was crowded to overflowing. Donald sat in front on the right side, behind the driver. Faaone, with her mother and sisters, sat on the left. Laughter and tears marked the departure.

Just a short distance out, the driver stopped the stage and got out to look at the engine. Faaone's company burst into song. The singing of the Tahitians usually had the power to delight Donald, but, unaccountably in this instance, he did not respond.

They had halted upon a stone culvert over a stream. From his seat in the stage, Donald looked over the railing of the bridge. The water made a rushing, melodious sound as it poured into a deep smoky pool that mirrored the broad leaves and pale blossoms of a huge wild hibiscus tree. Suddenly he experienced a sensation of complete isolation. He saw in the depths of that gold-streaked emerald pool not only the shiny silver shapes of nato but all the wonder and glory of Tahiti. And he was leaving her!

With a start, the stage rolled on again. How silly and uncalled for! After all, I am coming back to Tahiti, he reassured himself. But the queer cold thought let go only by slow degrees, as one after one the familiar and beautiful landmarks of the coast passed by.

187

15

❋

❋

❋

From the rim road high above Venus Point, Donald gazed over the curving lines of creamy foam across the blue channel to Moorea, miraculously ringed with pearl. Far down the winding shoreline, he saw a column of black smoke rising above the green. That would be the southbound steamer at the dock in Papeete. Sight of it brought him back to reality once more and inspired him with the assurance of success and the realization of dreams.

Their progress as they neared Papeete, with Faaone's crowd all singing again, elicited much excitement among the ever-curious natives along the road. They arrived shortly before noon. Donald had the driver stop the stage at the Hotel Diadem, where he and Faaone got off. Her family and the others would stay with various friends. Faaone warned them sternly not to drink too much, to save themselves for the wedding party to be held on the morrow.

"Well, we're here," Donald smiled at his bride-to-be. "You go on to Madame Reamy's at once. Tell her you need something in which to be married, and don't ask the price."

"All right, Donald," she answered softly.

"Tell Madame Reamy you need a complete outfit for ten days aboard the steamer to San Francisco. She'll know what to do. We'll get other clothes in San Francisco, for the States."

"But Don, this will all cost so much. Can you—we—afford this expense?"

"Faa, I haven't used a penny of my income in nine months. And remember the advance for my book. Yes, my darling, we can afford it."

"When—when will I see you again?" Faaone clung to him.

"Oh, we're bound to meet somewhere along the way. If we don't, then, here, at sunset. I must also have clothes. There are tickets to get, a stateroom to reserve. Then the marriage license and the church to see about. I'll be busy—and you will be too, if you mind me and get all the beautiful things I want you to have."

He kissed her and left her standing on the hotel veranda waving to him, rather wistfully he thought. He went first to the Chinese tailor where he ordered two silk suits and one of wool, the only bolt of this material the man had on hand. The tailor promised to work all night and have one suit ready early Sunday, the others by Monday afternoon. Donald bought one ready-made linen suit, the only thing that came close to fitting him, which he put on at once.

Next he assaulted the Chinese shoemaker, who, equally versatile, promised two pairs of handmade shoes by Monday and found a pair already made that would fit. By midafternoon Donald was dressed as he had not been since arriving in Papeete so long ago.

He went about the remainder of his errands with a vigor which belied the heat and the humidity. He was rather surprised when he did not run into anyone he knew, but then he had no time for the clubs and no doubt that was where his white friends would be on steamer day.

He was amused at the change in himself, in his mental poise as well as in his appearance. Not only was he a man around whom romance and tragic events had centered, he was also one whom the chances of life had marvelously favored. And he looked the part. His eyes were keen, no longer shadowed and aimless, and his face bronzed. There would be but few who would fail to perceive in him that something that clings to men of achievement. And no white man who saw Faaone would fail to envy him that exotic beauty! Donald could laugh at his pride and his vanity; nevertheless, this day he was thrilled by sensations that he had once bitterly renounced.

When late in the afternoon he left the steamship company, Papeete was at its busiest. Streets and cafés and stores were thronged. Donald went everywhere, leisurely, looking for Faaone. It would have pleased him to meet her at the humming Colonial or in the crowded Bougainville. He wanted to be noticed, and he wanted to share his strange excitement with her.

The whistle of the steamer, calling all passengers and crew to the ship in readiness for departure, brought what appeared to Donald to be the whole of Papeete's main street to the wharf. There he finally met Faaone and her worshipping contingent, waving farewell to anybody and everybody departing for Australia.

"Our turn next, darling," she sighed.

"But we go the other way," he replied.

"I think I would have liked our honeymoon more in New Zealand."

"We'll go there some day. Say, you're looking swell!— Faa, does all this mob know you're to be married to me?"

"Of course they do!" she cried. "Every person on Tahiti knows by this time. And I am the luckiest girl! To be married by a French priest to a white man!"

Suddenly her gay voice faltered and she turned her face to the sea and the departing ship.

"Don?"

"Hm?"

"Do you know, every girl, every woman, asks me if I am

190

coming back—how I can go at all. It would worry me if I could think . . ."

"Don't think, honey."

She turned back to him and looked up, her eyes black as night.

"Don, you *are* going to marry me tomorrow, aren't you?" she asked.

He sensed that she was serious. "Of course. What has got into you?"

"You do not know?"

"Know what?"

"Winifred has returned—on the ship which just sailed."

Donald exhaled suddenly, as if he had been struck a heavy blow.

"Yes, she is here," Faaone said, as if he had challenged her statement. "She is staying at the Diadem. I have seen her."

"Does she know—about us?"

"She has heard. I had the opportunity to tell her myself. Donald, she came back to get you. She will take you away from me. She is *so* beautiful, your white vahine."

"Nonsense!" Donald snapped. Nevertheless he was shaken by this, to say the least, unexpected turn of events, and she sensed it.

"You must see her, Don." Faaone put a hand on his arm. "It is only fair to her, and to yourself."

"Why must I? She messed up my life once already."

"Do you not see? I could never marry you unless I *knew* I was your choice after you had seen us both. Go—go now. She is in her room at the hotel. I—I will find you later on. And Donald —have no fear. I will not drink too much." She managed a wistful smile.

For a moment Donald did not reply, but stood facing her, looking down into her eyes, oblivious of the gay crowd that ebbed and flowed around them. Then he took her in his arms. "Darling Faaone, you know anything that ever was between

Winifred and me is over. It has been so ever since what happened at Tavarie's—perhaps even before! I think I loved you when I first saw you and spoke with you, only I did not know it. Now I do know it is only you I love. That is the way it will always be."

"Donald—" Faaone pushed away from him. "You must go."

"All right, if you insist. But it is to you I shall return."

Gently he released her, looked long at her, and turned away. Resolutely he made his way to the Diadem.

He found Winifred on a small porch adjacent to her suite. She was sitting in a chair facing the west, looking across the street to the bay and the lagoon, watching the golden sunset over Moorea.

"Win—" he spoke softly.

She jumped up, whirled, and came close to him, reaching out as if to take him in her arms. But she seemed to think better of it and, instead, held out a soft hand in greeting.

"Don! How are you? I'm so terribly relieved to see you alive and looking so fit," she began.

"Did you think I was dead?" he asked inanely, looking down into the dark violet eyes that once had so aroused him. He stepped back and ran his eyes up and down her trim figure.

"You look well, too, Win. No cane, I see."

"Then you *did* receive my letters. That is why I came. I was afraid you had not. I even feared you might really not be alive. Catherine Bellair was so evasive about you when she wrote, and she did not answer my last two letters. You did not write at all," she added reproachfully.

"Win— What was there to say? I had turned my back on the past, on America, on everything and everyone I knew."

"But what about your book? Your future?"

"Win—Faaone told me she informed you of our coming marriage," he replied, ignoring for the moment her mention of his novel.

"Yes, Don." Winifred's face was pale even in the waning

192

light. "Somehow it doesn't surprise me. I deduced from what Catherine wrote that you were living with her. And I knew how my Donald Perth would react to that—only with honor," she said with something of her old spirit.

"Then why did you come back, Win?" Donald asked bluntly.

"I came because I love you so very much, Don, a thousand times more than when you brought me here as your fiancée. I did not know then what real love meant. God knows, I have suffered for what I did to you. I hoped to find you alive. I hoped to take you back with me."

They stood and looked at each other. Donald thought how easy it would be to take this beautiful woman in his arms, this woman to whom he had once been engaged. He desired her—any man would—but . . . he knew now he did not love her any more.

"A man would be lucky—to be worthy of your love, Win," he said, lamely.

"You are worthy, Donald, and you need me. You can't stay here. You're going to be a tremendous success. I have money. I can help you a great deal. I would be proud to be Mrs. Donald Perth." Winifred's eyes sparkled with excitement and appeal. Her cheeks were flushed. Again she reached out to touch Donald's arms with both her hands. Donald looked at her sadly.

"No, Win. It's too late. Faaone and I sail for the States right after the wedding, on Monday's ship. You're right about one thing, though. I don't intend to bury myself any longer. Although—" he hesitated. "Although, we will come back to Tahiti, of course."

Winifred drew back, fury now in her eyes.

"So you're going to America, are you? To New York. To see your publishers. With a native wife—a poor one at that. What do you think *that* will do for your career?"

"I couldn't care less," Donald snapped. He continued, trying to control his anger. "Love is a one-way street, Win. It must be traveled by two people going in the same direction. When I was

193

in love with you, I was traveling alone. So were you, Win. Faaone and I are traveling together. She will never be a hindrance, but a help."

"You've developed into quite a philosopher, Don," Winifred said sarcastically, as she seemed to gain more control of herself.

"Perhaps I have," he replied shortly and turned to go.

Suddenly her hand was on his arm. He turned again to face her. "Don, I know when I'm licked," she said tremulously. "I'll be a good sport about it. May I come to the wedding?"

"Of course, Win." Donald stared at her. He had not expected anything like this.

She reached up and softly kissed him on the mouth. "That's for luck, Donald."

She turned away and walked to the porch railing, where she stood, shoulders squared, hands gripping the railing, silhouetted against the paling afterglow.

Donald watched her for a moment. Then, almost under his breath, he said, "Luck, Win," and turned and left.

Winifred stood at the porch railing, fighting back the tears until she heard the door close softly behind her. She waited a few moments, then numbly went into her room, threw herself prone on the mat-covered bed, and wept as if her heart would break. Break! It was broken, she thought. This was the utter end, the bitter end. She had irrevocably lost Donald, just when she had finally, she thought, become worthy of him and would in his eyes once again seem to be so.

When the tears would no longer come she lay there spent, a prey to bitter memories. Now she was alone. Her mother was gone, Donald was gone, and she had only herself.

She thought of the wedding dress she had been presumptuous enough to buy and bring along. Certainly there was nothing like it on this hateful island. What would she do with it now?

It was a long and bitter night she spent, listening to the whisper of the tropic breeze through the palm fronds outside, a witness to the specter of her broken dream. It did not matter to her that Donald had been living with Faaone. She was no moralist; how could she be? She remembered the night she had offered herself to Donald. Why hadn't he taken her then? Misguided chivalry, she supposed. But it had driven her into the arms of Tavarie.

She felt no shame about Tavarie. She knew that, somehow, when Donald would not have her, she had been a natural prey of the tremendous physical force within her. Her only regret was that, because of Tavarie, she had lost Donald—she was vain enough to think he would never have looked at another woman, even one as beautiful as Faaone, if she had not gone to the Tahitian.

She was honest enough now to wonder whether she had ever felt for Donald the passion Tavarie had roused in her, but it did not matter. She wanted him desperately. Had she given up too easily? Donald did need her, even if he did not know it. His sense of honor would prevent his leaving Faaone, but perhaps Faaone could be made to give him up. In the morning, Winifred decided, she would see the native girl.

With the coming of dawn, Winifred felt equal to the ordeal of the morning. She must face Faaone, and she must be proud and hold her head high. She dressed deliberately in her simplest yet finest clothing. She made certain which room was occupied by Donald and Faaone, then found an inconspicuous place where she could watch—and hope—for Donald's departure. Surely he would have things to attend to. Presently she saw him leave, closing the door softly behind him. She waited a short while, then slipped down the hall and softly knocked.

"Who is it?" Faaone's rich melodious voice came from within.

"Winifred, Faaone. May I come in?"

"Of course. Open the door. I cannot myself at the moment."

Winifred crossed the threshold and closed the door behind her. Faaone, in front of the mirror, was struggling with the hooks and eyes on a dress. It was obviously a new one, and though stylish enough, Winifred knew it had been made in Tahiti. Faaone turned to face her.

"I'm glad you asked me in, Faaone," Winifred began. "I have something to say to you—"

She broke off suddenly, silenced by something in Faaone's face—a savage expression, Winifred thought. But it was gone as soon as it had come; the great dark eyes calm once more.

"Faaone," Winifred began again, "you and I have a great deal in common. We both love the same man—but—Faaone, can you make him happy?"

"Why do you ask?"

"Don has just become a successful writer. He will be famous. He can go far—"

"And what you mean, Winifred, is how far can he go with a half-caste Tahitian wife—a poor one at that?"

"Yes, to put it bluntly."

"It is true I am not rich—but I am not ignorant. I am as educated as you. In fact, I do not know if you have as much schooling as I. I have lived much of the time with my mother's people, but I have not forgotten the white man's ways. I shall not be a hindrance to Donald."

"Perhaps you will not hold him back—that way—but . . ."

"Then, what is really bothering you is whether I will measure up socially, whether I will be accepted, because of my Tahitian blood. Do you think Donald cares?"

"I know he doesn't. He has said so. But you could keep him out of circles in which he should travel. If you love him . . ."

"And *you*, Winifred, you are acceptable everywhere! You, who though not married to a Tahitian—a native as you say—was discovered by Donald in the hut of one! I see nothing wrong in what you did. You could not help yourself. But it made a murderer of Donald. All my life I shall stand between him and any thought of that. If or when it should occur to him, and I know it does at times, I shall be there. And Winifred, do not doubt me,

I can make Donald forget anything in the world except me!"

Faaone's eyes flashed as she spoke, and Winifred recoiled more from that look than from her words. She knew at that moment that she had lost and turned away, walking quickly towards the window. Tahiti! How she hated it! She had been a fool to come back. She turned again to face Faaone. This was humiliating, and she would not be humiliated. Suddenly she knew what she would do. She spoke.

"Faaone, would you do me a great honor?"

"Yes—?"

"I brought with me a wedding dress, a beautiful thing. Would you accept it from me and wear it today? As a token that I wish you and Donald a great happiness?"

Faaone looked at her for a long moment with fathomless eyes. Then she said, "On one condition, Winifred. If you will come to my wedding I will accept. For if you come I shall know certain things—that you still love Donald, and that because of this you will not try to see him again. You will let him find his happiness—with me."

There was another long moment of silence. Then Winifred, without expression, walked to the door and opened it.

"Yes, Faaone, I'll—be there. And it shall be as you say. . . . Goodbye. I shall send my maid to you with the dress."

16

❋

❋

❋

There had been no formal arrangement for the wedding, yet it seemed to Donald that it had all been rehearsed. As one in a dream, he watched Faaone walk down the aisle to him on the arm of Bellair, who had been summoned on the coconut radio to give Faaone away. Colored shafts of light from the stained glass windows of the church illumined Faaone's dress. It puzzled him, that dress. Surely it had not come from Madame Reamy. Dimly he saw Winifred in the last pew. Winifred! He could not understand why she was there, but he admired her for the courage it had taken to come. Surely she and Faaone had talked. . . . But now Faaone was beside him, and nothing else mattered. He owed the rehabilitation of his life to her, and he was very proud.

After the ceremony they drove back to the hotel, where Dubrelle, the proprietor, was anticipating the wedding party with voluminous manifestations of delight—one long celebration until the northbound ship sailed!

Before delivering Faaone to her family and friends, Donald wanted her alone for a few moments. He escorted her to their room.

198

"Darling," she said as soon as they were alone. "The wedding —was it not beautiful?"

"It was, and so were you, Mrs. Donald Perth. Your wedding dress was also beautiful. Where did you ever find it?"

"It was a present that Winifred brought me from the United States."

"But—" Donald did not finish the statement. Winifred could not have brought with her a wedding dress to give Faaone when it was only yesterday in Papeete that she learned Faaone and he were to be married. No, Winifred must have brought the wedding dress all right, but to wear when she, herself, married Donald. What had possessed her to give it to Faaone? And why had Faaone accepted the gift? She must have known it was not meant for her. Best perhaps not to ask. Faaone was talking gaily about the wedding. Donald shook his head in perplexity and turned his mind to what she was saying.

"Don, I never even dreamed that anything like this could happen to me. I am happier than I have ever been in my whole life."

"I'm happy, too. And now that I can be proud of you as my wife, I can hardly wait to show you off in New York. You'll be a huge success, darling."

"Success?" The smile suddenly disappeared from her eyes. "Don, it frightens me—all that way across the sea," she whispered.

"It need not, Faaone. You must be glad that because of you I can lift my head again."

"Oh, I am, darling. But, sometimes, I begin to think—to see . . . You *will* bring me home to Tahiti? Promise me, Don."

"I promise."

"Soon?"

"In a few months. I thought we could live in Tahiti nine months each year."

"And will I always be your Reef Girl?"

"Forever, Faaone."

199

Dubrelle had promised Donald a wedding party to outdo and outlast all others, and he made good his boast. Faaone's dinner was one that would be talked about among the Tahitians forever. There were thirty courses. Donald tasted everything, and as long as he had any taste left he liked it all. There was singing and music and hula dancing. Faaone was a famous dancer of the hula, and Donald was drunk enough to ask her to dance it for him, but not so drunk as to be sorry at her refusal. The Tahitian hula was not the sort of dance, he decided, that one's wife should dance in public.

The hour came at length when the hilarity of the party and the throng of uninvited on the porch outside got a little on Donald's nerves, dulled and hazy as his senses were. Finally he took Faaone away from them. But in the morning, when he awakened and went downstairs, the party seemed to begin anew, if it had ever abated. When it finally ended, most of the celebrators had gone to sleep in their chairs or under the tables, and the northbound steamer had arrived from Rarotonga.

Donald had all his baggage taken on board to their stateroom; then he hurried back in a taxi to the hotel. Faaone was up, half-dressed, brushing her long hair. Her face was whiter than the petals of a tiare-tahiti flower. That singular pallor brought out her wide dark eyes in striking relief.

"Faaone, are you all right?" he asked, anxiously. "I let you sleep. . . . All our bags except this one of yours are aboard."

"I'm fine," she answered, her contralto voice a little husky. But she was languid, and it seemed as if she were trying to remember something.

"Let's get down to the ship," suggested Donald. "We'll have dinner aboard. Anyone who wants to—see us . . ."

He broke off rather haltingly, seeing that she was sweetly amenable but unthinking. He helped her finish dressing, and led her quickly down to the taxi, fearing she might ask for her mother and the others. She did not, however, and Donald concluded that if she thought about them at all it would be to know they were still sleeping.

Dusk had fallen. The electric lights flared. The taxi driver, turning into the main street, honked his devious way among other cars to the wharf. Donald helped Faaone up the gangway, and they were on board. Through the wide door of the salon, the last of another gorgeous sunset shone with dying fire. Purple clouds mantled Moorea. The lagoon shimmered out to the crawling white reef. Faaone followed Donald down the steps to the corridor, and he soon found their stateroom.

"Here we are, Faa," he said. "All set— We sail at dawn."

"I remember," she rejoined, gazing around the room. "This is the kind of stateroom I had when I came home from New Zealand so long ago— Don, I feel so strange."

"You'll be okay."

"I wonder." She rose from the couch, where she had sat down, to put her arms around his neck. "I'm glad it's over, my husband!"

"You mean your party? So am I."

She leaned heavily against him, without replying. He felt the slow heave of her breast, the beating of her heart. Gently he laid her down upon the berth.

"Rest a while, Faaone," he whispered.

He sat on the edge of the berth. In the shadow, her face could scarcely be distinguished against the pillow—but for the halo of black hair and the midnight eyes, Donald could not have told where it was. Her hands were cold and clung to his without strength. He wanted to say a hundred things, yet could only lean over her and lay his head against hers to kiss her temple.

When the bugle sounded for dinner, Donald rang for a steward and had some food and drink sent in. Faaone had little appetite; by coaxing her, however, he got her to eat a few bites —he was sure she had not eaten since the wedding dinner. After that she consented to walk on deck.

From the bay side of the ship the view was dark and mysterious. Only a few red lights from fishermen's torches, the sullen moan of the reef, and a faint gold in the west, low down along the horizon, gave substance to the void. On the wharf side there was bustle and din. The stevedores were loading copra and freight. Faaone stopped Donald by the rail to watch and listen. The cars came honking and rattling out of the huge shed to dump their bags of copra into the rope nets. The whistle blew; the nets swung upward and inward to the grind of the winches. Hundreds of half-naked Tahitians, brawny of arm and shoulder, toiled under the white lights. The moist air reeked with sweat and copra and dust and smoke.

Suddenly Donald saw Matureo and Punerie in the street. They approached slowly and lethargically. At the foot of the gangway they had to wait until the stevedores and members of the crew had descended. Then, with Punerie supporting Matureo, they labored up. Faaone fairly dragged Donald to meet them. Her mother, unable to talk coherently, embraced her.

"Well, Don," said Punerie, in English, "the stage is ready. So we have come to say goodbye. You will come back viti viti?"

"Yes, Punerie. Three or four months. Be sure to take care of our house."

"I will, sure." He turned to Faaone, still held fast in her mother's arms. "Faaone—Faaone, you be a good girl. . . . Come home viti viti."

Donald turned away from the farewell. Presently Faaone rejoined him, wiping her eyes. She watched until her mother and Punerie had passed out of sight through the gathering crowds. He hoped she was not disappointed at the failure of her sisters and friends to come to the boat—no doubt they had been bundled into the stage too suddenly and while too sleepy to remember what the trip to Papeete had been about.

Then Donald spied the Bellairs' car coming towards the wharf.

202

"Look, Faa. Here come the Bellairs," he exclaimed.

"I would like—to run," Faaone replied in a smothered voice.

"Don't. You'll miss something. They *are* genuine, no matter what else."

Catherine, cool and stylish in white, swooped down on them well ahead of her husband.

"Here's the bride!" she cried gaily, and she kissed Faaone in a way that proved her enthusiasm. "Faaone, you darling! I congratulate you, Donald. Faaone, I hope you'll always be as happy as you look lovely this minute."

When Bellair came up, he too congratulated Faaone and then turned to Donald.

"Congratulations on your reviews," he said.

"Reviews?" faltered Donald. "What are you talking about?"

"Haven't you seen the San Francisco papers?"

"No."

"Well, here's the *Examiner* and the *Chronicle*. They came in on the boat, but I didn't look at them until now. They rate your book with Melville's *Typee*. Of course, *we* all know *Faaone* has *Typee* backed off the boards. . . . I say, are you all right?"

"Yes, of course. It's just that I'm quite—staggered. Fact is, I haven't even signed the contract they sent me."

"Radio them from the ship tomorrow."

"I will, of course," said Donald as he took the newspapers.

They had strolled a little away from Catherine and Faaone.

"Don, I'm happy for you," said Bellair, suddenly solemn. "Long ago I was something like . . ." He seemed to shake himself, then went on. "I'm damn glad you're pulling out. Not many wanderers can beat Tahiti. Don't risk it again."

"But Bell, you know of course that I will come back—and soon." declared Donald.

"I have a hunch you won't. Since I've lived in the South Seas I get hunches. This one is straight. Once you go, you will never come back!"

Bellair usually red-faced, was pale, and he gazed with unseeing eyes at the copra schooners along the quay. Suddenly Donald realized that his friend was seeing in him—in his bright and alluring prospects—the dreams and possibilities of long ago, now forever gone. It was an unexpected, poignant moment, which Donald was at a loss how to meet. Whatever Bellair's tragedy was, although it had probably not begun in Tahiti, it would surely end here.

"So—goodbye, old man," resumed Bellair huskily. He wrung Donald's hand and rushed away.

"Goodbye, Bell. I'll be seeing you," Donald called after him.

Catherine then bade Donald farewell, gripping both his hands tightly in her own. "Goodbye, Don. Send me your book. Be kind to Faaone." She turned abruptly to follow her husband, stopping briefly to wave before she disappeared down the gangway.

Donald, with Faaone clinging to him, stood watching them depart. All at once an insupportable sadness assailed him.

"Faaone, let's go down," he said, leading her away from the rail. "No one else will come. We are tired, and it is over."

Faaone was silent, drooping. In the stateroom she began to undress, whispering to herself. Donald felt vaguely that there was something strained or unnatural about her, but he did not speak to her. Instead, with trembling hands, he opened the newspapers Bellair had given him. There, as Bellair had said, were the incredible words—"brilliant . . . remarkable . . . sensitive . . . Melville . . . Conrad . . ." If such reviews had appeared in the West Coast newspapers, they had been in the Eastern ones, too. A stupendous ecstasy flooded over him.

He turned to Faaone, wanting to share the moment with her, but apparently she had fallen asleep the instant her head touched the pillow. No wonder! He would not wake her. He, too, was exhausted. Despite his excitement, he was asleep almost before he had completed stretching out.

He was awakened by the slow, dull throb of the engines.

Dawn was stealing in at the porthole, casting a halo around Faaone's dark head.

"Hello, darling. Did you sleep?"

"Oh, yes, I just woke up— Don, the engines!" she cried, peering out through the small round glass.

"They woke me, too. It's ten minutes to six!"

"I must go up on deck," she whispered. She was fumbling with the buttons on her dress with frantic fingers. "Come, Donald. Hurry!"

She ran out of the room.

He dressed quickly. Rushing up on deck he found Faaone leaning over the rail. A line of native women stood under the wide eave of the copra shed. A few Europeans were congregating on the wharf. Officials in white uniforms walked up and down the gangway. On deck, passengers in dressing gowns strolled to and fro, idly peering over the rail.

"Don, do you see anyone?" cried Faaone eagerly, searching the crowd.

"None of your people. But Punerie said they were going home yesterday. I don't think they'll come, my darling."

"No! No!" moaned the girl.

The deep-throated steamer whistle pealed out, somehow chilling in the light morning air. He was leaving Tahiti. It was inconceivable. He watched the longshoremen loosen the great cables. He saw an officer come bounding up to the deck, carrying ship's papers in his hand. A crew of four stood by to haul up the gangway. The whistle bellowed again.

Faaone called low to him, but he did not catch her incoherent words. The cables came sliding across the wharf. The ship was loose! Donald strained his eyes to see the slow, widening inches between the dock and the hull. With a creaking of ropes and chains, the gangway came up.

He moved over to put his arm around Faaone. He felt her shaking.

"They—didn't—come," she whispered, to herself.

"There! The bow's swinging out, Faaone," cried Donald. "She's free— Hear the propellers! Wave, Faaone—wave, to anybody. We're leaving!"

But Faaone did not wave or answer. She hunched over the rail, transfixed. Donald held her, comfortingly, he thought, but his gaze was on the widening space between wharf and ship, on the waving Europeans, the motionless Tahitians, the dingy copra shed, the schooners at their moorings, and behind it all the grand green mountains and gold-flushed canyons.

Suddenly there came a miraculous transformation. A diffused sunrise burst through the looming cloud bank. The silver rims of the clouds, the rosy rents through which the sun poured, the faint rainbows dangling their feet into the foliage, the evanescent and celestial lights—all these suffused the shoreline of Papeete and the lagoon with a loveliness that tore at Donald's heartstrings.

He looked again at Faaone. She was taut as a strung bow. Her face was ashen and her fine skin quivered.

The ship turned into the channel through the reef, cutting off the view of the shore and the mountains. The moan of the reef filled Donald's ears.

Suddenly Faaone, with a cry, ran to the opposite side of the deck. For a moment, as he turned towards her, she stood poised at the rail, looking at him with devouring eyes. Then, swiftly, she turned to the sea. Wildly tearing off her clothes, she began to climb the ship's rail.

"*Faaone!* . . . For God's sake, darling! Are you mad?" Donald screamed and started toward her. She paused a moment to look at him once more, her great eyes terrible with grief and love.

"Come back to me someday, Don!" she cried.

Then she turned away and dove into the sea.

In a frenzy of terror Donald dashed toward her, to reach the spot only a second after she had leaped into the churning waves. He leaned over the rail to see her golden body cut the water cleanly and go under. Then, up out of the seething green and white she flashed, shaking her head until her long black hair spread in the windy wake of the ship. With her powerful stroke, she headed for the reef.

Desperate, heedless of the screams of the other passengers, Donald leaped over the rail. He jumped deep into the sea and, stripping off his shoes and clothing as he swam, set out after her.

The looming ship soon passed from his sight, and he found himself in the midst of a current eddying and churning out to sea. He saw Faaone draw rapidly ahead and noticed that he was getting out of line with her. For a while he breasted the current. Then, realizing that he was tiring and that he could never swim straight in, he swerved to quarter with it toward the outer edge of the reef. It was not far, and he thought he could make it. But the thunder of huge rollers filled his ears, and the current swept him farther and farther off his course.

The first slow heave of swell lifted him high. From it, he saw Faaone crawl out on the reef, nude and golden in the sunlight, waving something white—her last garment—at the retreating ship. She was waving goodbye to him.

The wave let him down, and the current, slower now, carried him toward the white maelstrom where the great rollers broke. He could just keep afloat. A dark and terrible shadow came between him and the sun—a shadow where there were no clouds. He had sensed it before, the haunting power the reef had over him. He would never leave it now, whether he died or, by some miracle, lived.

The sky grew darker. Almost dreamily he watched the bat-winged tupapa'u of death reach down to envelop him. Another wave lifted him and bore him reefward. Suddenly, he saw Fa-aone throw aside her garment and leap back into the churning waves. She had seen him. There was hope! Confounded, the tupapa'u drew back, hovering, waiting. Donald turned and swam away from the reef with all his waning strength. The great wave ahead of him lifted him ponderously to its crest, but broke just behind him. He swam desperately towards the next one, which was already looming high.

Then he saw the golden form flash into view just behind him. There was terror in her voice.

"Swim towards the wave as fast as you can—I will help you."

A new surge of energy seemed to invade his tired muscles. He swam more strongly with her beside him. The next wave loomed high but it did not crest, and they were out of danger for the moment.

"We must rest now," she said. "First you lean on me, then I will on you. We must go back through the waves. The current is too strong in the passage."

They clung to each other for what seemed an eternity.

"We must time it right," Faaone said. "Are you rested enough now?"

"I think so."

"Then follow me. The big ones have gone, and we have a little time before more come. Remember, we must swim just behind the first one and then under the next."

They swam back slowly toward the reef. The next wave, much smaller than before but still massive, lifted them and crested a few yards ahead of them on its way to the reef.

"Now swim towards the reef as fast as you can!" Faaone cried.

It seemed to Donald that they had gained pitifully few yards before the second wave loomed up menacingly behind them.

"Now *dive!* Dive under it—swim straight out, then up," she screamed.

Donald swam for what seemed an eternity before he burst into the sunlight, but the wave had passed and somehow he was still alive.

"Now, one more dive—then I think we can ride the last one in."

Again, an eternity of holding his breath. But now they were near the reef.

"See that channel there? We must ride the next wave over it, or we will strike the reef."

The next wave broke ponderously behind them, and a huge white wall of water came churning toward them.

"Put your arms up—aim for the opening!"

The wave roared over them. Donald was propelled forward with terrifying force. Any moment he expected to be dashed against the razor-sharp coral. He could see nothing but white foam all around him. Then, almost miraculously, the foam disappeared, and he found himself floating beyond the edge of the reef in water that was shallow enough to stand in. But where was Faaone? His heart almost stopped. Had the shadow of death come for her instead of him? He looked around desperately.

"I'm behind you, darling. You were perfect. Now you know how to swim on my reef." Then she was beside him as he clambered wearily onto a large, flat coral head.

She put her arms around him and held him to her.

"Oh, my beloved, I was so afraid. I never thought you would try to come after me. What a blind, foolish child I am! I almost killed you. Look, the ship has stopped. They will come back for us. I will go with you now, I promise!"

"No, my darling." Donald sat up, his voice strong and confident. "There are things more precious than fame or money, Faaone. I can write from here. Let the publishers come to us. I know now that you *are* Tahiti, that if you leave her you will die in your heart. I swear to you that we will never leave." And oblivious of the pounding surf, the rising sun, and the returning ship, Donald Perth drew his Reef Girl to his breast and fastened his lips to hers.

T H E   E N D